New Direction

Ron Mueller

Fiction Series

The Alex Evercrest Series
The River Front
The Girl on The Grill
Missing
Maggot
Racist
Votive Candles
Windy City
Country Road
Pool of Blood
Sins of the Daughter
Body Parts
The Skull Collector
The Vanishing
The Shadow Fighter
Moonshine
Grief's Trajectory
The Magic Touch
Northern Lights
New Direction

A Brian Oneil Novell
Hawaiian Phoenix
Moon Curser
Death Broker
Hawaiian Princesses

The Problem Solver Series
Solutions
Drug Lords
Border Crosser
The Problem Solver Collection

Imagination by Courtney Huynh and Chloe Parker

New Direction
By: *Ron Mueller*

Around the World Publishing LLC
4914 Cooper Road Suite 144
Cincinnati, Ohio 45242-9998

ISBN 13: 978-1-68223-945-2
ISBN 10: 1-68223-945-4

Distributed by Ingram
Alex Evercrest Model By: Pi03@ShutterStock
Cover Picture by: Nataliia Korzhenevska @ShutterStock
Cover by: Ron Mueller

Ron Mueller

New Direction

Table of Content

Ron Mueller

Chapter 1: The Change in the Air

The trip to Brazil to arrest Cristiano and the subsequent gunbattle was a catalyst that made Alex's adoption of Aurea the crucible of change that Alex had expected it to be. She recognized it as such and on her return to Cincinnati, she had let Matt know her feelings. She was seeing the adoption as a way to add new meaning to their lives.

Matt agreed with her that adopting Aurea was a positive life changing event for him as well. He confided in her that it gave him new energy and a desire to see Aurea grow up happy and empowered. He wanted to give her hope for the future the way his father had given it to him.

One morning over breakfast, Alex voiced her desire to move back to Evanston and give Aurea the chance to experience growing up much as she had. She recognized that the way her parents had raised her was the way she wanted to raise Aurea.

Matt thought that it was a great idea and said that he probably could easily get hired there as an EMT.

Alex said that she wanted to change their lives for the better. She then added that she wanted to buy the marina where the Golden Goose was docked, and she wondered whether he would be interested in running the marina.

Matt smiled and said that he would be more than happy to do so. He chuckled and asked if he could become the captain of the Golden Goose.

Aurea piped in and said that she could help in running the bait shop, and she could be a deckhand on the Golden Goose.

Alex nodded and said that she wanted to make the Golden Goose a money maker by taking people out to go fishing.

Matt said that he was going to start taking lessons to become a certified captain.

Aurea asked if she could take lessons too.

Alex said that all of them could take lessons together. She added that it would be great to run the marina as a family affair.

She contacted Dexter the owner of the Marina, and asked if he would consider selling the marina to her.

Dexter replied that her timing was right for him, and he could think of no one better to sell it to. He asked if he could continue to work for her and help her get the hang of managing the marina. He added that he was ready to take more time off and travel a little and play golf more often.

New Direction

Alex said that she would welcome his guidance but that she wanted to have Matt do the actual hands-on management. She added that she wanted to make the Golden Goose a money maker that would help her pay for the marina.

Dexter said that he would get the paperwork to sell the marina to her ready. He asked if he could hold the mortgage until it was paid off.

Alex said that she wanted them to remain friends and would feel better if the mortgage was held by a finance organization because she planned to accelerate the payment so that she would have a clear title as soon as she generated the money to pay for it. She added that her mother had always advised against having a friend hold a mortgage if you wanted to have that friend for life.

Dexter laughed and said that the advice was a good one and it sounded like her mother, who always was all business.

His comment caused Alex to call her mother and let her know what she had in mind.

Rose-Anne was ecstatic when she heard what Alex had in mind. She said that both she and Russel would love to have Alex, Matt and Aurea live in the house. It would bring new life to it, and she was willing to make breakfast and lunch forever. She asked how soon Alex was planning to make the move.

Alex replied that it would take a few months to get everything organized and arranged. She added that if Aurea were to spend the summer in Evanston the transition might go faster.

Rose-Anne let out a whoop and said that she would love to have Aurea lead the way. She added that Russel would spoil her by taking her fishing every weekend.

She, Matt, and Aurea went to Maui on a two-week vacation where she was faced with more change. Linda and Lorie no longer the two little girls that she had rescued from the forest of Pennsylvania, asked for her support as they ventured into the business of being private investigators. Their request and subsequent discussions sealed Alex's decision to open up her own private investigative service as part of the move to Evanston.

Her offer to make them junior partners in her new venture in a private office in Evanston was eagerly accepted.

She enrolled the two in finding an office location within five miles of the marina.

Annie, Linda, and Lorie's mother thanked her for taking the two under her wings. She added that she liked that fact that the two were planning to have an office in Oahu as part of the venture.

Alex said that she was going to have an office in Evanston, would have an office in Cincinnati and now one as well in Oahu. She added that the Oahu office would be out of the apartment that Linda and Lauri were renting and the one in Cincinnati would be out of her house. This would let the two get started with a minimum of overhead.

She said that she was making the move to Evanston and setting up the main office there.

New Direction

On her return to from vacation, she offered Trey, her long-time work partner and Johnnie, her internet wizard, partnerships in the investigative service. She would have liked to extent such an opportunity to Bill and Trevor who had supported her during her entire career in Cincinnati, but she knew the two had been discussing retiring, buying a place near Lake Cumberland, and enjoying fishing and golfing.

Once the picture of what she had in mind came to her, she began to list the things she needed to get done to make it all happen.

She left Aurea in Hawaii with her mother and father who were coming in for a vacation at her Maui beach side home. Aurea would fly home with them when their vacation came to an end.

Aurea thought it was a great way to make the move to Evanston. She said that she was eager to live there and go fishing out on the lake.

Alex got all the paperwork prepared to resign her position. She came in and was going to share her decision but was surprised that the Chief called all five of them into his office.

The Chief held up a set of papers and said that they were his retirement papers. He said that he would stay on until the next Chief was identified.

He looked at her and said that he was putting her name in as his replacement.

Alex shook her head and held up the papers in her hand. She said that they were her answer to his question, and the papers she was holding said no to him putting her name in to replace him.

She looked at Trey and asked if he had any interest in the position.

Trey shook his head and said that if the papers she was holding meant that she was leaving the department, then he would most likely see if he could become a bus driver or a security guard at the river front.

Trevor laughed and said that would be a step up that would be hard for him to make.

Bill gave Trevor a shove and said that he understood Trey's position.

Alex smiled and said that she had a position in her new venture as her partner and asked whether that met the low requirements that Trey was shooting for.

Trey beamed a smile and said that he would love to continue being her backup work partner.

Alex nodded and said that they should all plan on going to lunch wherever Johnnie decided they should go and during lunch they could all take a moment and describe what they were planning on doing in the coming years.

New Direction

The Chief looked around and said that it seemed that the department was going to face a serious change and that a discussion over lunch would be a great way to sort it all out. He suggested that they spend the morning getting organized and at lunch they would share what was happening with each of them.

Alex suggested that she, Trey, and Johnnie go to a huddle room, and she would share what she had in mind.

Bill said that he and Trevor would go to another huddle room and get on the internet to see if they could find a place near Lake Cumberland that would interest them and be acceptable to their wives.

Once in the huddle room, Alex shared her vision of running a detective service from Evanston. She asked if the two of them would be interested in being senior partners with her and having Linda and Lorie be two junior partners.

Trey said that he would jump at such an opportunity. His only consideration was that he wanted to make sure that Lindsey would also want to do it. The only hang up was that Nolan was looking for a place in Cincinnati to live and had rejected living at home.

Alex suggested that Nolan could house sit her Cincinnati house once she had moved to Evanston.

Trey nodded and said that would allow he and Lindsey to rent their home and have a little income until their business started to generate an income.

Alex looked at Johnnie and asked him if he was interested in the venture.

He smiled and said that he was ready to let Mary know that they were moving to Evanston.

Alex's phone rang. She answered it because she knew it was Linda calling.

Linda excitedly let her know that she and Lorie had found three potential office locations. She was sending the pictures of the places. She added that she and Lorie had rated the places in the order that they thought was the nicest office area to the least liked one.

Alex thanked her and after making arrangements to look at the places she hung up.

She sent the pictures to Johnnie and asked him to put them on the large screen.

Johnnie took a few moments and then he put the first office choice up.

The three of them went from office to office and agreed that Linda and Lorie had made the right decision on the appearance of the offices.

Trey pointed out that the least liked one was the one that was within walking distance to the marina. He pointed out that most of the parking area could be turned into a garden. The interior could be redone to make five large offices along the front and have several meeting and work rooms along the back.

New Direction

The entrance and reception area could be spacious and have the coffee and refreshment area incorporated.

Johnnie added that a flower garden around the building would greatly help its appearance.

The three of them decided that the first office area in the high rise with a great view of the lake still held the number one position. Choosing it would depend on the price and conditions of the contract.

Office choice number two was not as impressive and the only thing it had going for it was all the great restaurants that were within a five-minute walk.

Choice number three was down to its lease price and remodeling cost versus the other two.

Alex smiled and said that things were working out as good as she had hoped they would. She asked if calling their business, *"Evercrest, McGregor, Smith and Obrien Partners, LLC"* was acceptable.

She got a thumbs up from both Trey and Johnnie.

She then asked Johnnie where they were going to have lunch.

Johnnie smiled and said that they should have it where they first had it when he was looking for logs floating down the river.

They left the huddle room and shared their lunch location.

Trevor laughed and said that he and Johnnie had to sit with their backs to the river because the last time they faced the river, the two of them had spotted a body in the tree that had floated by and ended up being a case that came to them.

They all agreed that they would not look for logs floating down the river.

Alex let the Chief know that they were ready to go to lunch.

Chapter 2: The Office and the Marina

The Chief led the way into the restaurant where they were led to a table set up in a private room. He went over to the window and closed the shades. He turned and declared that there would be no looking at the river to see if logs were floating down stream. That got a quiet "Hurrah" from both Johnnie and Trey and a "you got it" from Trevor.

After the meal orders were in, the Chief let them know that he had put Bill's name in as his replacement and that he had gotten an early confirmation that it was a great choice.

Trevor declared that he was being sabotaged. He and Bill had just agreed to look at three properties near Lake Cumberland in which they were interested.

The Chief smiled and said that his announcement did not change anything about their plans. He continued and added that it would only change the timing since Bill would be made temporary Chief within the week and the assignment would be for a year until his replacement was in place and trained.

The arrangement would give the department time to look outside of the department for a replacement. He smiled and said that there was also a significant bonus attached to the position. He said that he was sure the bonus would make a significant down payment on the property they were looking at.

Trevor smiled and said, "In that case, I will encourage Bill to say yes."

Alex laughed and asked if that meant that the Chief was going to get out the fastest of them all and if so, she was extending an invitation to him to come to Evanston to go fishing out on the lake.

Bill looked around and said that he thought that closing out his career as the Chief of the Cincinnati Detective unit would be a great honor. His only regret was that the best detective team was leaving as he took over.

He added that he and Trevor had found three potential homes near Lake Cumberland that were of interest, and they were wondering which one they all thought might be the best. He put the pictures of each down on the table.

They all gathered around to take a look.

Alex looked at the three. She pointed to the largest house that had four bedrooms, a detached four car garage that was on five acres of land that bordered the lake. She said there was only one choice, and it was not a matter of cost, it was a matter of keeping their wives happy.

Trevor laughed and said that for once he agreed with her and he turned the other two pictures over.

He then asked if she had anything to share about what was going on in her life.

Alex nodded and said that she would like to introduce "*Evercrest, McGregor, Smith and O'Brien Investigators, LLC.*" She pointed to Trey and Johnnie and said that they had agreed to move to Evanston, Illinois and go into business with her.

Bill asked if the O'Brien were the two little girls she had rescued from the Pennsylvania forest.

Alex nodded and said that they were no longer little girls but sharp shooting women eager to put the bad guys in front of the judge.

Trevor let out a gasp and said, "just think of the negative influence you had on them."

Alex smiled, nodded, and replied, "I hope to get them qualified and operating in as safe a manner as I possibly can. I personally wish they had chosen to follow in the footsteps of their mother and had become artists but that did not happen."

Bill added that she had kept them all safe in some of the most dangerous confrontations, so he was sure that she would do the same with the two. He then asked her if there was more to her move than setting up a private practice.

Alex nodded, smiled, and asked if he had been listening to her phone calls. She said that indeed the biggest news for her was that she had made a deal to buy the marina where the Golden Goose was anchored, and it was part of the deal. Even better was that Matt was going to manage the marina and be the captain of the Golden Goose.

"Now that the use of the Golden Goose is free to you, do you think that Bill and I could join you on another fishing trip," Trevor asked as he shook his head up and down.

Alex laughed and said that if he paid the for the gas he and Bill could go out any time they wanted to go.

Bill chuckled and asked how much the gas cost for a trip.

Alex replied that it cost close to six hundred dollars.

"Wow, the Golden Goose is not so golden," Bill exclaimed.

"Well, she will be making money when she goes out on fishing trips, and I hope to have her going out often. The marina is currently a breakeven business after paying the current owner a decent income." It will give Matt a raise and he is looking forward to being the captain of the Golden Goose.

Johnnie gave a laugh and said that maybe on slow days at the office he could be a deck hand and do a little fishing on the side.

"If you get away with that, then I will have to do the same," Trey piped in.

Alex said that she had recruited the two junior members of the business to do an initial search for a sufficiently large office space for the five of them. She added that she had three pictures to share and wanted to get an opinion from all of them.

She put down the picture that Linda and Lorie said was their first choice. She pointed out the scene of Lake Michigan from the lobby area and from the office that she said was her favorite.

Trevor commented that it certainly beat the current office area they all shared, and it was indeed an impressive office.

She then put down a picture of the second office area.

The Chief said that it looked OK, but he wondered what it offered besides the space.

Alex replied that Linda had highlighted that it was surrounded by great restaurants.

"All you need is a good donut shop. So that one goes way down on the list," Trevor chided.

Alex then put down the last picture.

Trevor shook his head and asked why that office had even made the list.

Alex said that it was only a few minutes' walk from the marina.

Bill spoke up and said that the proximity to the marina trumped the other two locations.

Alex nodded and said that she agreed but she was going to look at all three before making up her mind. She asked Trey and Johnnie if they wanted to go along with her to scope them out.

Trey shook his head and said that he trusted her to make the right choice.

Johnnie nodded and said that he agreed with Trey.

The Chief commented that he and Mary-Anne were planning to stay put in their current home, but they planned to visit all the countries National Parks and take the cruise from Seatle to Alaska in the coming few years. He said that it had been tough for him to decide to retire but now having listened to everyone's plans he felt much better and was looking forward to it. It felt good to get out feeling like he was on top.

The days following the lunch meeting and discussion filled by the activities in the office, getting Nolan situated to live in the house to take care of it, setting up the office area in the house for Linda and Lorie and getting ready to move to Evanston kept Alex going full tilt. She felt a little overwhelmed and was grateful that Matt had quit his job to manage the details of making the move.

Linda and Lorie flew into Lunken and then a day later the three of them flew on to the Chicago Executive Airport near Evanston to look at the office choices.

The first office location was only five minutes from the airfield. They met the realty agent and went on a tour of the space available.

Alex had to admit that it had a great view, and the space felt new and fresh. She inquired about the cost and the rental agreement. When she heard the monthly fee and the conditions in the lease agreement she had second thoughts but said nothing.

She felt that the cost was more than she wanted the new business to absorb.

The three then went on to the second potential office location. They were less impressed with the office area, but the financials were much more attractive. But again, Alex felt that the cost was still too high.

They took a walk and verified that the place was surrounded with several good restaurants. They chose one that advertised the best and freshest sushi. During lunch they discussed the first two office areas.

Alex commented that the first office area was hands down the nicest but was also very expensive. She made the point that the partnership did not yet have one customer, and the first office was where a very successful business would move up to. She commented that the second office was sufficient, and the restaurants added a nice secondary benefit but again it would be a stretch. She added that she was going to let the last location determine what she would do.

Lorie commented that maybe she and Linda had not done too well in selecting the office spaces to look at.

Alex shook her head and said that both spaces were good ones, and she reiterated the fact that she would wait until they had looked at the last one before deciding what they should do next.

After lunch she called the last realtor and arranged to meet her at the final location.

They got out of the taxi and looked around the rather large parking lot and the single level red brick building. The realtor was not there so Alex suggested they walk around the edge of the property. They walked around the back of the building and back to the parking lot. Alex commented that more than half of the parking lot could be turned into green space. She said that it would make a great flower garden and outdoor sitting area.

The realtor arrived and after the introductions they all went into the building. It had a large reception area and then what Alex thought of as a too narrow hallway the length of the building. There were already five offices along the parking lot side of the building and several meeting rooms on the other side.

Alex liked the feel of the building and the fact that it was only a few minutes' walk from the marina was what made an OK office area attractive to her. She remembered Bill's comment that the location was the primary thing to consider. She asked about the cost and lease terms.

The realtor hesitated for a moment and replied that the owner would prefer to sell versus lease. She stated that the asking price was seven and a half million dollars.

Alex thought for a moment. She said that she wanted to walk through the building one more time. As she walked she estimated the cost for widening the hallway, renovating each office, and eliminating half the parking lot and making it into a flower garden. She figured it would cost at least a seven hundred fifty thousand dollars.

She came back to the lobby area and said that she would offer six million, three hundred thousand dollars and would close the deal immediately if the owner accepted the offer.

The realtor answered that she would check with the owner to see if he would accept such a low offer. She walked out of the building to make the call.

Lorie asked why Alex was making the offer.

Alex smiled and replied that it was all about the location and the fact that she could spruce up the place to make an acceptable office space into a great office space with a beautiful garden area out front.

Linda asked if she thought there was a chance that the owner would accept the offer.

The realtor returned and asked if Alex was related to Rose-Anne Evercrest.

Alex said that was her mother.

The realtor nodded and said that the owner was familiar with her mother's very positive impact on the local community, and he said that if it was her daughter making the offer he would accept six million five hundred thousand.

Alex smiled and asked when the papers would be ready to sign.

The realtor replied that the paperwork could be ready by the following Wednesday.

She asked whether Alex wanted the keys to the place so that she could make plans for any changes she had in mind.

Alex accepted the keys and said that she would be bringing in an interior decorator and a contractor to look over the place.

After the realtor left, Alex led Linda and Lorie through the building again. She walked to the end of the hallway and pointed to the back corner office and said that it would be hers. She then walked by the next two offices, said they would be Trey's and Johnnie's offices. She then walked into the next office and asked which of the two of them wanted it.

Linda replied that it would be a great office for her.

Lorie smiled and said that left the last one for her. She pointed out that hers was closest to the lobby and would make it easy for her to greet their customers.

Alex shook her head and said that she was going to hire a person to be the receptionist and office manager.

She pointed to the back meeting rooms and said that she was planning to widen the hallway and some of the meeting room space would be taken. She also wanted the reception area to be enlarged slightly to accommodate a refreshment area and to give the receptionist a dominant presence.

Lorie commented that Alex seemed to be prepared for this third location.

Alex replied that it was all about location and this was the place that had the location.

Alex then suggested they walk to the marina and then they could take a taxi home where her mother was planning a braised lambchop dinner.

New Direction

She added that Aurea was staying with her grandparents for the summer. She was planning to stay over the weekend to do some fishing with her and stay long enough to close on the purchase of the marina and their new office building.

She commented that during her move to Evanston, the two of them would have time to make their move to Oahu and get situated. She hope that soon the business would get its first customer, and they would all be gainfully employed.

Ron Mueller

Chapter 3: Bittersweet Goodbye

Leaving Cincinnati and the detective unit took on a bittersweet aura. On the one hand Alex looked forward to the move, but she had many fond memories about her time in Cincinnati. It was the place where she had come to a maturity that she felt was the one she had always hoped she would achieve. It was the place where she and Matt had realized they were meant for each other. It was the place where she had developed her skills and had learned to handle the subtle race discrimination and had flourished in spite of it. She had been able to solidify the detective unit into a great working partnership.

Now after she had decided to leave, she had been offered the position of Chief of Detectives, but she knew that it was time for her to make the move back to Evanston. Taking the promotion, though it was very attractive would take away from her new goal of focusing on family.

She was pleased that Bill would realize his dream of becoming the Chief of Detectives. This was something he had wanted when she had first come to Cincinnati. It provided a great secondary sense that it was the right decision.

She thought it interesting that Trevor, who from the very beginning had given her constant harassment, had chosen a young black female policewoman to be his partner. She teased him about trying to replace her.

Trevor shook his head and said that he had selected the best candidate, and it had nothing to do with color. He added that his new partner was much smarter than her.

Alex shook her head and said that her willingness to be his partner put that statement into question. As she bantered with him, she realized that one of the things that she would miss was the daily exchange between the two of them. His teasing had kept her on her toes. She was sure he would develop his new partner into a top detective.

On her final day in Cincinnati Matt drove her to the airport. He went in with her to the check-in counter. The two of them were walking to the security area when a trumpet blared out "Honor and Arms." Alex was surprised to see all of the Detective Unit present, Chief Johnson, and his boss the Police Department Head. It stopped her in her tracks. It was a surprise that she had not anticipated.

The Police Department Head stepped forward and praised the outstanding work she had done over the years.

Matt held her hand and gave it a squeeze.

She had tears in her eyes. She felt the sendoff all the way to her heart. Suddenly she felt weak. She wanted to turn and go back to her house. The thought about what she was leaving overwhelmed her. She was frozen in place, but she felt like turning and running away.

Bill broke the spell by stepping forward and letting her know that she had enabled him to realize his dream. He added that he would make sure the success that she had insisted on would be part of the detective department culture that he would make sure was held up.

Alex nodded her head and said that she was overwhelmed and honored by her sendoff. She said that in the future she would be on call to provide any help that the detective unit might need or ask for. She added that she had grown up professionally on the culture and atmosphere that Cincinnati offered and would miss it greatly.

She knew that the news cameras were present so she made sure to mention that Chief Johnson had been her mentor and that his replacement Bill Danson would be a great Chief of Detectives. She then praised the Police Department Head as a person who had supported all of them and had done a great job in his role. She knew she was praising a person that had initially been against her taking a lead role.

She then said that there were so many great people, and she would miss them all but the person she would most likely miss the most was Travis Carter who every morning made sure she raised her defenses by giving her a hard time. He was the one that made her seek the hard solutions to many of the cases that she had solved. If she had failed she knew that she would not have been able to continue in her role because he would have made life at work really hard to handle.

She gave Matt a kiss on the cheek and whispered that he should have warned her. She gave a wave to the crowd and walked toward the security area.

She was intercepted by a gate security agent and escorted through a separate area and out to the escalators leading to the gate trams. Being escorted allowed her to recompose herself. She chose to walk to terminal B instead of taking the tram.

The short flight to Chicago gave her just enough time to decompress. She felt great about the sendoff and felt great about the experiences she had in Cincinnati. She decided that she had to make sure that her new venture gave her the same feeling that she had experienced in Cincinnati. She felt lucky to have Trey and Johnnie joining her in Evanston. The two were her bedrock foundation that she knew she needed as she started up a new business.

She landed and was walking out to get a taxi when she saw her mother, father and Aurea waiting for her as she exited the security area.

New Direction

Aurea rushed forward and they exchanged hugs. Aurea said that it was great to have her mother finally moving in permanently to the mansion of her rich grandparents.

Rose-Anne gave her a hug and said that her daughter was constantly reminding her and her father about how rich they were. She gave Aurea a hug and said what they were rich in was having such a great daughter and granddaughter.

Russel came over to her and said that he hoped that she was traveling light because they had driven her Jaguar to pick her up.

Alex pointed to her small roller bag and said that it was everything she had.

They walked out to where the Jag was parked. Her father asked whether she wanted to drive. She shook her head and said that she would sit in the back seat with her favorite daughter.

Aurea laughed and asked where the other daughter was.

They all climbed in and drove into the city and up along the lake front toward home. This was the home where she had grown up. They were driving past the University where she had received her undergraduate and afterwards her law degree. This was the lake where she had fished almost every Saturday with her father. She knew that she was coming home and that she would give Aurea the same opportunities that she had unconsciously experienced.

On the way home, Aurea let her know that she and her grandfather had gone out to the office building that she had purchased to inspect the renovation it was undergoing. She said that the two of them had worked with the landscaper and done a layout for the part of the parking lot that was to be a flower garden. She then said that the interior decorator had taken them for a tour of the work being done internally and her office was almost done.

Aurea continued to list the things that were going on and she ended by saying that Dexter had volunteered to take them out fishing, but she had chosen to go out on the "Minnow" with her grandfather because it was more fun fishing from it than the Golden Goose.

Rose-Anne looked over her shoulder and said that Alex had just received an update from the expert on everything that was happening. She then added that lunch was going to be a salmon salad and there would be chocolate cake for desert. Dinner was to be lake trout caught by Aurea and it would be accompanied by a large baked potato smothered in a butter cream sauce of her own making.

She added that Alex would have time to visit the office redesign and get an idea if Aurea and her father had the right design for the garden area.

New Direction

The busy, full schedule for the day was just what Alex needed to make her transition. Things were moving at the pace that she wanted them moving and it was providing the sweet flavor of change that she needed to follow her emotional departure from Cincinnati. She knew that Matt would be leaving Cincinnati the following day and driving their black SUV loaded with all the last-minute incidentals that they had forgotten to pack out with the moving van.

Lunch was light and just what she needed to carry her through the day. She agreed to take Aurea with her to review the construction progress at the office location. She asked if anyone else wanted come along.

Russel said that she was taking the expert, and he did not need to come.

Rose-Anne said that she was going to focus on getting dinner prepared and then sit by the pool area and relax.

Aurea was excited to be leading the tour and said that she had a few surprises that she wanted to highlight. She carried the drawing that the landscaper had provided. She added that they had become friends and that she deserved a good tip for having incorporated the idea of adding a wisteria trellis on each side of the garden.

Alex laughed and said that the wisteria trellis was Trey's idea.

Aurea smiled and said that she had stollen it and presented it to the landscaper who thought it was a good idea.

The landscaper had suggested buying four mature wisteria plants that were as high as the trellis so that the trellis would be quickly covered.

Aurea said she had agreed, and that plan was in progress. She added that she had asked to have the edge of the property lined with alternating yellow and red roses.

Alex asked if she had made any changes with the inside office design.

Aurea shook her head and said that she figured that working on the yard area would be OK but doing anything in the office area was off limits.

Alex smiled and said that if she thought of any improvements to the inside design she could voice them on this tour.

Once they arrived, Alex suggested they first take a walk around the yard area and get a feel for the good work that Aurea was leading.

Aurea led the way and excitedly pointed out the work that was already done in getting the roses planted. She added that her grandmother had suggested the roses that were being planted. When they got to the area of the parking lot that had been removed to accommodate the flower garden, she pointed out where a bench would be placed at each end of the garden and the trellises that were already up. She pointed at the oval garden area and said that yellow roses would be at the center and would be surrounded by red roses similar to the ones her grandmother had at their house.

She stopped and asked what Alex thought about the work on the yard.

Alex smiled gave Aurea a hug and said that she was doing great. She looked at the brick exterior and said that they should get the brick pressure washed so they would look new.

Aurea agreed and asked if she should contact someone to do the pressure washing.

Alex nodded and said that would be a great idea. She then took Aurea's hand and led the way into the office building.

She was pleased to see that the hallway was already done and each of the back meeting rooms had the glass partitions put in. She walked back to her office where she could hear work going on.

The contractor stopped the work and greeted her. He pointed around and asked if the decor and wall covering were what she had been expecting.

Alex looked around and commented that it was the best office that she had ever worked in. She especially liked the fact that all the file cabinets would be pulled out from the wall behind her desk. She commented that the shelves above the file cabinets made the office impressive. She could envision her desk and the meeting table in the room. She decided to contact he interior decorator and make sure that the desk and table that they had initially selected were still the ones that fit the decor.

She complemented the contractor on having the meeting rooms along the hallway almost done.

He commented that those rooms did not pose the challenge that the office areas did. He said that his guys were being stretched by the interior designer in getting the offices to be to her standards.

Alex nodded and said that she was most likely the person who was causing him the problems because she had insisted on the offices being the best. She added that after the next two offices, she would like to make the receptionist area the focus so that it would be ready for whomever she hired to run the office area and to be the receptionist.

Aurea asked if Alex had any idea who the receptionist would be.

Alex shook her head and said she would be spending the coming week interviewing people for that position.

Aurea asked if it had to be a woman.

Alex shook her head and replied that it could either be a man or woman but women where the ones that historically had filled that position and she wanted a very experienced person to set up and manage the office so it would most likely be a woman.

Aurea nodded and said that she hoped whoever was chosen would be a person that got along with her.

Alex said that she would make sure that would be one of the criteria for who she selected. As she walked out holding Aurea's hand, she asked her if she was ready for lunch at their favorite pizza parlor.

Chapter 4: Office Manager

The two of them decided on a combo pizza that had pepperoni, green pepper, and pineapple chunks on a thick layer of cheese. A sliced tomato salad as a side served to balance the pizza. To drink she had iced tea and Aurea chose lemonade.

She let Aurea know that she was going to spend the rest of the week looking for an office manager.

That afternoon she asked her mother's office support if they had any person in mind that was looking for a job and got several references. All were women. She hit pay dirt on the third call when she talked with a Marisa Eberly. They agreed to meet for lunch the next day for an interview.

Alex chose a restaurant that had a second-floor patio area and had a menu she enjoyed. She arrived a little early so she could get a table that was in the corner farthest from the entrance area.

When Marisa arrived she was pleased to see that she was a person who did not try to look un-aged. She wore a practical black suite outfit and had a confident walk. Marisa was half a head taller than she was and was on the slender side. She had blue eyes, white hair, and a distinctive narrow nose. She had thin silver column earrings that swayed as she walked. Alex put her down as a person who had been very good-looking and who still was very attractive and was aging well.

Marisa introduced herself and asked what Alex would like to know.

Alex suggested they order first and then they could get into the opportunity she thought might be of interest.

She ordered an eggplant salad, black mussels and for desert she chose mango and passionfruit cream layered crepes and to drink she chose an iced tea.

Marisa chose a shrimp salad, fried mushrooms, chose a chocolate cake for desert and iced tea.

Alex shared the fact that she was opening an office that would house five detectives. She let Marisa know that she also had purchased Wilmette Harbor Marina that was within walking distance from the building that she had just purchased to be the office of "*Evercrest, McGregor, Smith and O'Brien.*" She let her know that she was also an Investigative Marshall for the state of Illinois and had licenses to practice in all other states.

She then asked Marisa which professor she had worked for at the University.

Marisa smiled and said that before she shared her background she needed to ask if Alex was related to Rose-Anne Evercrest the lawyer that her friend worked for.

Alex smiled, said that she was, and her father was a professor at Northwestern University.

Marisa nodded and said that she had supported a professor at Northwestern until he got a position at the University of Illinois in Champaign-Urbana. When he left, there were no other positions she wanted to fill at the university, so she was out looking on the open market. She shared that she had more than twenty-five years of experience as an office support and before that she had worked in a bakery for a few years. She had never married, had no children, and lived not more than two miles from the restaurant where they were having lunch. She added that she was still unemployed and that the situation that Alex had described sounded interesting to her.

Lunch arrived and the talk turned to more personal topics.

Marisa asked why Alex was moving back to Evanston.

Alex explained about adopting Aurea and wanting her to have similar experiences that she had when she was young. She shared that going fishing with her father had been a highlight of her upbringing and the marina had always held an allure for her.

Marisa smiled and said that fishing was one sport that she had also enjoyed all her life and still did. She went fishing almost every weekend when the weather was good, and she had even tried ice fishing. She added that ice fishing was much too cold and was not for her.

Alex knew that the top pay for a senior office support was roughly sixty thousand dollars. She made an offer of seventy-five thousand dollars and watched what the reaction might be.

Marisa stopped with her fork midway to her mouth and asked if she had heard correctly.

Alex repeated her offer and said that there would be times when she should expect some long hours and hours that were not part of the workday.

Marisa smiled and said that the offer was very generous, and she was ready to start that very day.

Alex said that after finishing their desert the two of them would go to the building she had just agreed to buy, and she would share the changes that were happening to make to the grounds more attractive and to the interior to make it a top-of-the-line office.

When they walked out to the Jaguar, Marisa commented that it was a beautiful car.

Alex said that it had been a gift for her high school graduation from her parents. It was an old car at that time, but her father had recently had it painted black and had all the technology updated. It ran like a charm, and it was her prized possession.

New Direction

Marisa smiled and said that it was nice to have such generous parents.

Alex nodded and said that they were a big part of the reason she was returning to Evanston.

When they arrived at the office Marisa took in the one-story red brick building that was wrapped in windows. She looked out at the garden with the two trellises and wisteria vines. She noted the roses that seemed to run around the border of the property. There were two persons pressure washing the brick and all the cement work. The part that was done made the brick seem new. The place was going to look new, and the place was going to look grand.

Alex led the way around the property border.

Marisa commented that the roses really set the yard area off.

She added that she liked the fact that most of the parking lot was now a flower garden.

Alex surprised her when she said that the parking in front of the building would be assigned by office location. That meant her parking space would be the closest to the front door and Alex's would be the farthest from the front door. This surprised her but she kept quiet. She was beginning to think of Alex as a super person to work for.

They entered and Marisa walked the hallway listening to what Alex was having done to the interior. She learned that all the offices including her entrance office would have similar furnishing and the interior would have a common theme.

Alex said that the first thing that she needed to get done was to get all the official paperwork masters set up. She asked if Marisa was ready to set up a functioning office on the ground in Evanston, a home office in Cincinnati and one in Oahu, Hawaii.

Marisa smiled and said that she was getting surprise, after pleasant surprise. She was certainly going to enjoy her new position. She laughed and said that she would need to go to Oahu so that she could properly set up that office.

Alex liked the interaction that she was having with Marisa. It spoke well to the atmosphere she wanted to have in the office.

She invited Marissa to join in on a fishing trip on Saturday and that she would meet her daughter Aurea who had the last word on her staying hired.

Marisa said that she would love to come.

On Saturday morning, Matt, Alex, and Aurea left the house early in the morning and rode the black Jaguar to the harbor. After parking they carried their things to the Golden Goose. A few moments later they watched as Marisa parked her grey Honda and walked up the pier.

Marisa looked at the white yacht with its white canvas cover over the back deck in awe. She had always wanted to go out on such a beautiful boat but had always figured she could not afford to spend that kind of money.

Alex greeted her and said that breakfast was being served and asked Marisa what she wanted with her pancakes.

New Direction

Marisa sat at the table in the galley and watched as the person who had been introduced as Matt made pancakes and fried eggs. She said that one pancake, one over easy egg and one sausage and a cup of coffee would be great.

Matt looked up to the parking lot and announced that the rest of the group going fishing had arrived. As soon as they were onboard, and he asked them if they wanted breakfast he would get everyone ready to go out.

One of them said she wanted breakfast but the other four said they had already eaten.

Matt got them situated. He then gave them all safety instructions, had them each put on and adjust their life vests. He then asked them to keep the vests close by but let them know that they did not need to wear them.

He pulled in the boarding ramp and pulled in the lines tying the Golden Goose to the pier. He climbed up to the conning area and maneuvered out of the harbor.

Marisa said she remembered some of the news reports a few years ago that included the Golden Goose but none of those reports had any of the details that she was now curious to learn about. She listened as Aurea shared what she knew about the attack on the Golden Goose by a racist trying to kill everyone on board.

Once he was out to the fishing site, Matt turned off the engine and proceeded to get the five customers that had paid for the fishing trip, fishing. He helped bait their hooks with the bait they chose and if they asked he cast their line.

Alex watched as Aurea helped Marisa get her pole ready. It turned out that Marisa was a person that loved to fish and didn't need any help, but she listened to what Aurea had to say and it was clear that the two were getting along.

Everyone had their lines out in short order.

The fishing was good, and everyone was catching fish.

Matt was busy making sure the fish were put into the holding tanks where they would stay alive until they were cleaned.

He got the grill going and put on hamburgers, sausages, brats, ears of corn, carrots, and broccoli. Earlier he had made two large coolers filled with tea and lemonade. There were also soft drinks and beer and wine in the refrigerator.

He made a point of letting everyone know that it was all you could eat, and drink and lunch would be available from ten thirty to noon.

After catching three nice bass, Marissa decided that she would have a glass of wine, sit under the canopy, enjoy the view, and watch the other people fish. This was the dream fishing trip that she had always envisioned, and she wanted to savor it.

Alex joined her with a glass of lemonade and asked if she was enjoying herself.

Marisa said that she was and that she had learned a ton about the person she was working for from Aurea.

Alex smiled and said that she was sure that Aurea had embellished the stories that she had heard.

Marisa shook her head and said that if even half of it was true it was still an amazing story. She thanked Alex for inviting her out fishing and said that doing something like this had always been on her bucket list.

Alex said she was happy to have helped get it checked off. She then invited Marisa to a dinner of freshly caught fish at her house.

When they returned to the pier, Alex led the way to the fish cleaning station and said that everyone cleaned the fish they had caught. She was quickly done with the three fish she had caught and then looked over to see if Marissa needed any help.

It was clear that Marisa was a fisherman because she had her three cleaned in record time and didn't need any help.

Aurea had caught three large lake trout and was working hard to get her fish cleaned.

Both she and Marisa grabbed a fish and cleaned them.

It was early afternoon and they all agreed to go to home, shower and then spend some time by the pool.

Marisa said she would go home, take a shower, and then come over and join them at poolside. She smiled and added that she had heard from Aurea that her grandparents were rich and didn't know it.

Alex made sure that Marisa took an extra fish home, and said that it would be only her, Matt and Aurea at the house and they had plenty of fish in the refrigerator.

Marisa drove home in somewhat of a daze. She stood under the shower and thought about the turn of events.

She had been at a low point looking for a job. She had found that most of the jobs on the market were really looking for younger workers. She had watched the eyes of the people doing the interviews and knew almost immediately that she was not being considered.

Her interview with Alex had been totally different from the beginning. She knew immediately that she would take the position if offered and the monetary side was not even in her thoughts. When the salary offer had been mentioned, she was shocked. It was more than she had ever made and more than she had expected to be offered.

The fishing trip had taken her over the top. She watched the inter action between, Matt and Alex and knew that the two enjoyed a marriage that enriched both of them. And their daughter Aurea, clearly adopted, was a treasure. She was fun to talk to and was clearly in love with her parents.

Marisa knew that her friend in Alex's mother's office was super supportive of her boss. She had nothing but good things to say. She had also been supper supportive of the pro bono work that her office did.

New Direction

As she drove up the drive to Alex's parents the house, she felt that her old Honda would be out of place.

She was met at the door by an older distinguished looking person who introduced himself as Russel Evercrest and led her through the grand family room to the pool area where everyone was gathered.

She was surprised to be introduced to a Trey McGregor and his wife Lindsey and a Johnnie Smith and his companion Mary Higgins. She learned that they had arrived that afternoon. The two couples were visiting the homes they planned to move into.

Alex came over to her and said that Johnnie had been a long-time biking partner in Cincinnati and that the homes the two of them had in Evanston made biking to work something that she planned to do. She added that Trey was planning to join them each morning.

Marisa said that she lived in the wrong location to join them, but she would try biking into work to see how that felt.

Aurea came over to her and asked if she wanted a tour of the mansion that she lived in.

Rose-Anne overheard her and said she would give her a tour of the house that was not a mansion though it was large and more home than she had ever wanted.

The tour cemented for Marisa that the family was very close, and that Aurea had become its new center of attention. She was impressed most by the family room with its six-foot-high fireplace hearth. The elevated hot tub with the water cascading down into the pool was the second most impressive feature. What made the tour fun was the running commentary by Aurea that kept emphasizing, "Rich and don't know it."

Chapter 5: Lightning Fast Start

The following Monday, Marisa drove into work and parked in the first parking spot. She looked behind the car at the flower garden that seemed to have flourished over the weekend. She really like the fact that she had the parking spot nearest the front entrance. When she walked in she found that her desk had been moved from the left side of the lobby where it had previously been located on Friday and it was now on the right side of the entrance. It was clear to her that a refreshment area would be to her right and behind it was the room that held seven four high filing cabinets. This arrangement clearly put her in command of the office building. She felt a surge of energy as she thought about the role she was being given.

A few moments later, Alex arrived, said good morning, and walked back to her office. A few moments later she returned and suggested that they go out shopping for computers, printers, and business phones. She led the way to her Jag and then drove to a local computer store where she ordered six laptops and six printers. She arranged for delivery that afternoon.

Marisa wondered what her role was on the shopping spree.

Alex then drove to a leading phone supplier and ordered six Apple fifteen phones. She had each one activated and made ready for use. She contracted for professional business coverage and global services.

Marisa commented that she had not been part of such a shopping spree in her life. She wondered if everything was going to be a whirlwind.

Alex laughed and said that she hoped not but she wanted everyone in the company to be able to begin work on the first day in the office. She said she wanted the appropriate contract and other paperwork needed to sign up a new client ready as soon as possible. She commented that they would need the paperwork on official letter head with *"Evercrest, McGregor, Smith and O'Brian, LLC"* ready by the afternoon. She asked Marisa if she could get that done.

Marisa smiled and said that current technology would let her get the first set of documents out with no problem. She would get examples from her friend in the law office and modify them, as necessary.

Alex nodded and said that she was meeting her mother and Aurea for lunch at her mother's pizzeria. She planned to order a quick salad and iced tea and then get back to the office to meet with Trey and Johnnie.

Marisa said that she was looking forward to lunch and finding out how to keep up with her mother from Aurea.

Lunch was the most relaxing event that the two of them had done so far that day.

Aurea provided the light mood that the two enjoyed as she talked about fishing with her grandfather on the weekend.

Alex reminded her that Matt wanted to go fishing with her too.

Aurea replied that the two of them were going out on Sunday because on Saturday, he had a fishing trip planned on the Golden Goose.

Rose-Anne said that on Sunday evening she was going to serve a spare rib dinner and was inviting all of the members of *Evercrest, McGregor, Smith and Obrien* that wanted to come over.

Marisa said that she would love to come and would be thinking about it all week.

Alex asked Aurea if Marisa qualified to remain employed in her office.

Aurea was quiet for a moment, nodded her head and said that she fished like a pro, cleaned fish like a pro, and she liked cookie and cream bars so that certainly made her a keeper.

Marisa laughed and said that she was glad to have made it past the toughest part of being hired.

Alex returned to the office and parked in her spot. She noted that Trey and Johnnie had parked in their designated spots. As she and Marisa walked in they were met by the two.

Trey commented that his office was a beauty and that he had never sat behind such a grand desk. He felt more like a tycoon than an investigator.

Johnnie nodded and added that he felt that he had moved from a utilitarian desk to an office that was meant for a pillar of high society. He added that it was a long way from sleeping in the woods next to the highway to where he now lived in Evanston.

Trey let her know that the contractor said that his and Johnnie's office was done and ready for use. Each office had a few electrical covers and other minor things that needed to get done.

Alex let them know that computers, printers, and phones would arrive that afternoon. She asked Johnnie to work with the internet provider to set up an office network. The center of that network was to be in the office across the hallway from his.

She then asked Trey to get in contact with Linda and Lorie and learn all he could about the case that the two had identified. She wanted to understand the scope of the case and how the three of them could be of help.

"So much for enjoying a casual week as things get started up," Johnnie joked.

Alex nodded and said that getting a first case almost immediately had surprised her as well, but they should all embrace it and see how they could make it work to their advantage.

Marisa asked what kinds of snacks they would like her to stock up the refreshment center with.

Alex suggested lots of fruit.

Johnnie added that brownies were always appreciated.

Trey said that they were used to a morning donut of some sort.

Marisa said that she would go to the grocery store and stock up on a variety of items and get their feedback on what she selected. She chuckled and said that she was going to make sure to include plenty of cookie and cream bars for her most important boss. She said that she would arrange for the delivery of a water cooler and daily delivery of the morning donuts. She said that she was going shopping, turned, and walked out to her car.

Johnnie looked after her and commented that Alex had selected a very capable support for the office area.

Alex agreed and added that she wanted Marisa to be the office manager, receptionist, and records keeper. She would have the same compensation that they all had as far as sharing the spoils of the cases they solved.

A couple of hours later Johnnie walked into Alex's office and let her know that the computers, printers, and phones had all arrived. He and Trey were going to unpack everything and set things up. He added that the internet guy would come in the middle of the week to get the internal internet set up.

He then said that he was going to need a more powerful computer if she wanted him to be the same magician that she had enjoyed in Cincinnati. He let her know that in Cincinnati, he had enjoyed a very powerful computer that had great speed and a huge storage capacity. He had been able to set up identities inside of it that allowed him to play sleight of hand games with other computers he was trying to hack.

Alex nodded her head and said that she likely had access to such a computer via her role in the lieutenant governor's office.

Johnnie said that would work but he would need to set up shop near that computer.

Alex asked how much the computer he had in mind would cost.

Johnnie said that he figured it would cost around ten thousand dollars.

Alex looked at him, smiled and said, "having a magician working for me is more expensive than I thought it would be. She smiled and said that she wanted a one-year pay back on the computer."

Trey walked in with a printer, lap top and asked where she wanted her gadgets.

She took the phone he handed her and pointed to the credenza where she wanted the printer to be placed.

New Direction

Trey commented that he had put all the printers and computers in all the offices and out in the reception area. He added that they should agree on the pass codes for each computer and get them protected as much as possible from the likes of Johnnie.

Johnnie laughed and said that so far he had not found anyone that was that great at hacking. He suggested that they each pick a five-letter password that had three letters, one number and one symbol.

Alex said that hers would be ACE1!.

Trey said that maybe he should be ACE2?.

Alex said that her password was her initials so his password should be TCM1~. And Johnnie's should be JBS1$.

Johnnie asked why she had chosen a dollar sign as his special character.

Alex laughed and ask him if he was the one asking for all the money to spend on a special computer.

Trey smiled and asked why she had chosen a squiggle for his special character.

Alex shook her head and said that symbol was one of her favorite ones and he was her favorite partner.

Johnnie asked if he was her second favorite partner.

Alex shook her head and said that he was her number one magician.

The contractor knocked on the door and said that his crew was going to be working in the back rooms and would be making quite a bit of a racket and was wondering if he should continue as planned.

Alex said that his work was the priority so she and the rest would find another place to work. When the contractor walked out, Alex picked up her new phone and put in the first person on her phone list, Matt. She then called Matt to see if the Golden Goose was available. Matt let her know that it was booked for Friday and Saturday but was open the rest of the time. She looked at Johnnie and Trey and asked if they would like to spend the time working from the Golden Goose.

Johnnie nodded and said that it would make things easier to get everything, he planned to do done.

Trey agreed and said that he always felt comfortable on the Goose except when she was getting shot at.

They were on the way out when Marisa returned. She said that she would unload her things, after that she would offer some refreshments to the contractor and his crew and then she would walk over.

Alex let her know that one of the activities for the afternoon was to set up their phones with all of their work contacts.

Marisa looked at Johnnie and commented that though the work for the day sounded boring, the work environment was going to be pleasant.

New Direction

When they arrived at the dock, Alex saw her mother's van. She asked Matt about it and found out that she was supervising the building of the Golden Goose Restaurant kitchen and service area. Alex smiled and asked how the supervising was going.

Matt commented that she was making a very positive difference and was teaching the builder about setting up a kitchen for a master chef. He laughed and said that the builder had called in the designer and connected her mother to her. He said that the designer was learning a lot about keeping fish cleaning areas separate from meat preparation areas and how each area should be easy to clean after each fish or specific piece of meat was processed. He added that Rose-Anne had also insisted in separate vents over each cleaning and stove area. He was not sure of the cost implications, but he trusted that it would work out to benefit them. He then said that he needed to get back to the office to make sure the store was operating smoothly.

Alex focused on setting up her phone. She had just finished what she considered her first pass when she saw her father walking toward the Golden Goose with Aurea. They were both carrying pizza boxes with the distinct logo of "Evercrest Pizza is the Best." She put her phone away and went down to the peer and gave Aurea a hug and took the three pizzas she was carrying.

Her father said that he had heard from his boss that she was not cooking anything that evening, so this was his version of cooking for everyone.

Marisa helped get everything ready. She added that she was going to leave after having a piece because she had a bike she was picking up. She added that she had scoped out the route that she planned to ride to work.

Alex suggested that she ride to the marina because the work for the next couple of days would be on the Golden Goose. She asked Marisa to see if the bike shop had a bike rack that she could buy to put outside of the office.

She was just sitting down with Aurea when she saw Matt and her mother walking down the pier. She went over to the gangway and waited for the two of them to come onboard. She gave her mother a hug and said that after she got her "dinner" she should come and share the improvements that she had made to the layout of the new restaurant's kitchen and serving area.

Rose-Anne gave Russel a hug and laughed when he said he had made dinner as promised. She took a slice of her "Ham and Extra Cheese Royal Pineapple, and a slice of "Cheese, Cheese and Cheese" and went to where Aurea, Matt and Alex were sitting.

She was excited to share the improvements that she had made to the kitchen and cooking areas that she had insisted get added.

She also wanted to share that she had been hired by the kitchen designer to review the draft drawings for three kitchens that her company was getting ready to build.

New Direction

She added that she had negotiated for free improvements to what was being built for them as part payment for the consultation.

Alex smiled, looked at Aurea and said that now she should begin to understand why she acted like she did.

Aurea nodded and said that she had chosen to stay with her grandfather because he was for taking it easy and getting ready to go fishing. The two of them had put new line on their reels and had selected the lures they were going to use. They had also decided to go out on Wednesday as well as on Friday.

Matt spoke up and asked if there was room in the boat on Wednesday for him.

Aurea got up and went over to him and gave him a hug and said only if he brought a good supply of bait.

Matt said, "deal" and returned her hug.

Johnnie had listened to the exchange and commented that he would be begging to go but his boss had given him a huge workload that was going to keep him busy the rest of the week.

Trey sighed and added that he too had a huge workload, but he was really looking forward to going out fishing on Sunday. He asked that Aurea not catch all the fish in the lake.

Aurea laughed and said it must be a tough boss that the two of them were working for and she hoped not to suffer the same fate when she grew up and went to work.

Alex shook her head and said that if working on the Golden Goose was so bad, she might have to think about a better place for them to suffer.

She said that they should all plan to meet at the office in the morning and then after a brief walk through they would walk over to the Marina and begin working.

Chapter 6: Knolton's Golden Goose Marina

During the morning walk through, the contractor pointed out that his team was nearly done with the three offices for the senior partners. He pointed out that the offices for the two junior partners were not far behind and the reception area was near completion. He estimated he would be done with everything inside of two weeks. He added that the exterior was pressure washed and an upgrade of the gutter system was scheduled for that afternoon.

Alex thanked him for his update. She turned to Johnnie and asked about the connection to the global internet and the internal internet.

Johnnie let her know he was meeting the representative for the external internet connection at ten that morning and he was working with that same group to set up an internal internet. Each of them would have three levels of protection. He said that he did not want anyone to easily hack into their system.

Alex laughed and said that the only hacking that would go on would be done by him. She suggested they all walk to the marina and work on the Golden Goose for the rest of the day.

She led the way and as they walked onto the property she pointed to its sign and said the name would be changed to read Knolton's Golden Goose Marina and Restaurant. She looked at her watch and said that their new office was only a seven-minute walk away. She entered the bait shop and was greeted by Dexter.

Dexter smiled and asked how the conversion of his old friend's office building was going.

Alex replied that the close location of his friend's office building to the marina had been the key attraction, and the office layout and size was the icing on the cake. She added that she had looked at two other very nice places that were only a few miles away that were nicer, but it was the location near the marina that made the difference. When the work going on there was over it would be as good of an office as the other two and it would only be seven minutes from the marina.

Dexter reminded her that they were closing on the marina that afternoon. He asked if by chance he could host a celebration party on the Golden Goose on the coming weekend.

Alex put a frown on and said that would not be possible because she was holding a party on the Golden Goose on that very day, and it was booked for fishing expeditions on Friday and Saturday. She then smiled and said he and his friends would be very welcome at her party.

She added that she would only need a list of everyone he wished to share the celebration with, and he would need to make sure they had the best bait possible for that fishing trip. She wanted everyone to enjoy the celebration and come back in with as many fish as they were allowed to keep.

Dexter came over to her and gave her a hug and said that selling to her was one of the greatest joys that he had. He asked if he could give her a ride home at the end of the day.

Alex shook her head and let him know that the team would be working from the Golden Goose for the rest of the day and then again on Wednesday. They had each ridden their bike's to work and would ride them home that evening.

Dexter smiled and said that she had fooled him by walking over from the office.

Alex nodded and said that she had wanted to walk over to get a feel of how long a walk over on a bad day would take. She then let him know that Marisa, the support that he had met, would be checking with him what he wanted for lunch.

She then led the way to the Golden Goose where she gave Matt a hug. He said that he was ready to sign for the property and he knew that her mother was once again going to be inspecting the construction of the restaurant and this time she was going to take Aurea with her during her construction inspection.

Alex smiled and said that Aurea was learning from one of the best.

Marisa spent the morning getting business documents created and sent out to Linda and Lorie.

She then went around and asked what Mexican lunch item each person wanted. She walked up to the bait shop and got the choice from Dexter and the young person he had working there. She called Rose-Anne and got what she and Aurea wanted and then called all the choices into the Mexican restaurant. She let everyone know that lunch would be delivered at high noon.

Rose-Anne and Aurea arrived for lunch and came onboard.

Aurea got a big hug from all of them.

Alex let the great feeling of having the whole family participating in making the transition from Cincinnati to Evanston such a positive affair soak in. She felt very good about the decision to leave the Cincinnati detective unit. Matt came over and gave Aurea a hug and asked if she was ready for her fishing trips.

Aurea was the one that was the most excited about working at "Knolton's Golden Goose Marina and Restaurant" and said that she was looking forward to the two of them riding into work on their bikes to the marina where she would help him run the place.

Matt smiled and said he was looking forward to having her help. He asked her if she wanted to be his deck hand on Friday and Saturday and help the guests in preparing to fish.

Aurea looked at Alex and asked if that would be alright.

Alex nodded and said that would be a great way to learn the business.

New Direction

For Alex, the move was a huge change in all of their lives that she had yet to take in. She was used to the routine that she had set up in Cincinnati. She wondered how she was going to handle setting up a new routine as she established her own business. So far everything seemed to have a positive feel. The missing element was how Linda and Lauri were going to be an integral part of the business.

She knew that Trey and Lesley had found a home near where she lived, and he had joined the morning bike ride in.

Johnnie had had found a place only a few blocks away from her house. This let her know that in good weather they would all be riding their bikes in to work together.

So, the change seemed to be going in the positive direction.

The closing for the marina took place that morning without a hitch. Matt was now the primary owner, and she was his silent partner.

He had let her know how great it made him feel. He said that he missed his EMT team members but did not miss the EMT work experience. The experiences at the marina were all on the positive side with no blood and guts. He added that the business finances for both businesses were set up and the money needed to cover the transition costs was in hand so that made him feel that they were over the main hurdle in the finance area.

Linda called and shared that they had been hired by Navy Lieutenant Lydia Murray to investigate the potential murder of her friend by a Navy Lieutenant Lyle Halloway.

Alex said that the first order of business was to get them both sworn in as marshals in Hawaii.

She worked with Marisa to swear in Linda and Lorie.

Marisa was the witness and then she sent them a picture of their badges.

Linda said that she would call back when they had more details about the case.

The following morning Alex was still at home having breakfast with her mother and Aurea and was surprised when she heard that Linda, Lorie, and the Navy Lieutenant Murray were on a flight to San Diego Naval base to apprehend a fleeing Lieutenant Halloway.

She said that she was going to swear them in as deputies in the State of California and would send out their badges to their emails and phones. She asked if there was anyone with them that could act as a witness to their swearing in.

Lorie said that Lieutenant Murray agreed to be the witness.

Once the swearing in was over, Alex asked if they had their protective gear with them.

Lorie said that they both had their protective gear with them and were wearing it.

Alex wished them luck and said she wanted to hear from them after the arrest.

When she got the next call, she was in a discussion with the contractor.

Trey, Johnnie, and Marisa were at the reception entrance area discussing how they would be working together.

Alex went up to where they were sitting and put her phone in speaker mode and asked Linda to describe how the arrest had gone.

Lorie said that she had been shot by Lieutenant Halloway. She then said that Linda in the process of disarming the Lieutenant had shot him in his right foot and left knee with his own weapon. Neither of them had time to draw their weapons. She laughed and said that the Lieutenant was threatening to sue them for shooting him.

Trey commented that it seemed odd that the Lieutenant had acted so violently. He added that perhaps Linda should see if there was more going on than just his flight from the attempted drowning of his victim. He asked if they had checked on his other duties and if there might be some sort of other activity going on.

Linda thanked him for the suggestion because it had not occurred to her.

Johnnie spoke up and said he would see if he could find some sort of money trail.

Linda added that the Kevlar vest had saved Lorie and that they had agreed that it would be hard for them to leave their apartment without wearing it.

Alex reminded Linda that she and Lorie were on the hook to paint something about the case that they were on the verge of solving. She suggested that they identify the Oahu law group that they should use for the murder trial, and they should identify the Oahu judges they would prefer.

Alex asked them to get Leilani, and her two detectives, now located in Oahu, updated on the case, and see how they might be of help. They probably knew which lawyer and judges they preferred.

The next day she learned that Lieutenant Halloway was flown back to the Oahu Naval base where he was under guard. She learned that he was formally arrested and had found a lawyer to represent him and vowed to sue Linda for having shot him.

Linda shared Leilani's recommendation of lawyer and judge and got Alex's agreement to utilizing both. She closed with saying she would report any additional significant information as it occurred.

Lorie shared the fact that she had a huge purple bruise and that it was already changing to a putrid yellowish and grey. She added that sitting in the apartment's hot tub had helped and the pain was down to a mere mosquito size or maybe a mole hill.

Alex laughed and said she was well aware of the cycle of pain after having been shot and hoped that Lorie would not be surprised next time.

New Direction

Johnnie came on and said that he was sure that there had to be more people involved in a redirection of government equipment, weapons, and munitions because he had found an offshore bank account that had three billion dollars in it under the Lieutenant's name. He pointed out that was not an amount a Lieutenant could possibly accrue on his pay.

Trey came on and suggested that there had to be a person on the Oahu end, another on the airplane, and at least another at the San Diego base. He suggested that they find out all the sites where the cargo plane flew and check those locations for the people receiving the plane.

During subsequent discussions Linda and Lorie agreed that they should hand over the smuggling case to the Navy and let the prosecuting Navy Judge Advocate handle the details of that case.

Alex suggested they meet with that person to see how *Evercrest, McGregor, Smith and O'Neill, LLC* could be of help.

They agreed to work with Johnnie and the IRS to get their reward for finding the money in the offshore bank account. Alex pointed out to them that once the Navy learned of the account they would want that money, so it was important to get the Oahu IRS agent engaged first and as quickly as possible. She added that Johnnie knew how to ensure that they got the maximum finders reward.

She made the point that the money would come to the *Evercrest, McGregor, Smith, and O'Neill LLC*. Each of them and the firm would get one sixth of that money. She asked how the two of them felt about their share that would be fifty million dollars each. She added that the two of them had provided the firm a solid start and that allowed all of them some breathing space as they started up.

Alex shared that Johnnie was continuing to investigate where the smuggled goods ended up and in doing so had found one destination where most of the smuggled goods ended up. The location was in California. He had determined that it was a seemingly legitimate business. It was owned by a holding company that distributed survival supplies around the world. His additional digging identified that the goods went to several individuals that showed up on a list of gunrunners. The holding company's money ended up in overseas accounts in numerous countries.

She said that she wanted the two of them to work with Johnnie and when they had a solid understanding of that part of the smuggling ring they would decide how to handle it. She added that EMSO's objective would be to get their share of the money Johnnie was uncovering in offshore accounts.

Alex got off the call and asked Johnnie for the addresses of the businesses involved in the distribution of the smuggled goods and the persons who were involved.

New Direction

Alex asked Trey if he was ready to head to California and do some gumshoe investigation of the individuals and the businesses.

Trey smiled and said that as always he would be with her and have her back.

Marisa was surprised when Alex asked her to check on flights to California and asked her to see if there were any private flights from the Executive airport. Alex wanted to know how much they cost and compare that cost to two first class tickets to San Francisco. She had additionally added that she preferred the private flight if it was with a with a service that had been in the business for several years.

Marissa spent a couple of hours making the arrangements. She let Alex know that she had booked the flights out of Ohara because she needed to follow up on two potential private services.

Johnnie got a call from Lorie asking about the San Francisco end of the smuggling business. He let her know that Alex was planning to go and do some on the ground investigation and that she should talk to her.

Alex got the heads up from Johnnie about a call from Lorie. She decided that having Linda and Lorie participate with her and Trey was a good way for she and Trey to work with the two of them.

She asked Johnnie to dig into how the smuggled goods were being distributed and who was handling the goods. She figured that it could be a very significant network. She asked him to see if there were other branches of the military involved with the San Francisco connection.

Johnnie began by getting into the main San Francisco smuggling business computer and looking at incoming money that corresponded with the flight schedule of the Oahu Navy transport flights. He spotted consistent cash flows of four thousand and nine hundred ninety-nine dollars each day in the weeks after each flight. These cash flows came from six banks in the San Francisco area. When he traced those accounts he was able to locate the banks that had transferred money in. The source banks yielded the names of a half dozen individuals.

He drew out the network and realized that he had uncovered a significant weapons smuggling operation. He shared that he had not yet gone to the next level of exposing the network or all the sources of the weapons. He stated that he was sure that more than the Navy was involved. He pointed out that the largest source was most likely the Army.

Lorie was impressed with his ability to hack his way through almost every firewall he encountered. She asked him how he did it and said she wanted to learn some of the ways. She asked for and got several of his hacking bots and said she was going to learn how to do some of what he was doing.

Johnnie laughed and said that he did not want to corrupt such a young lady.

He then shared to the team the company's San Francisco address and the person who he suspected was the kingpin of the distribution operation. He let them know that the person did not have a police record, but he was surrounded by armed bodyguards who had a checkered past.

Alex thanked him for the great work and said that she and Trey would meet Linda and Lorie the next morning in San Francisco. She added that by then she would not be surprised to learn that he had more detail available for them to work with.

Johnnie diligently kept tracking the flow of money associated with the smuggling operation. It became clear to him that it was a bigger operation than just the Hawaii connection and it involved more than just the Navy. He kept being surprised by the source of the money. He indeed found the connection to the Army smuggling operation. Then he found the connection to the Airforce smuggling operation. He did not find any to the Coast Guard but did find a connection to the National Guard. It had tons of missing equipment.

He found it a little harder to figure out where all of the goods were going but he figured it was just a matter of time. He knew that his ability to hack was going to make him and his business partners very rich. He smiled at the thought of the days when he had slept under over passes and bridges. He knew that Alex had changed his life in every way possible.

Chapter 7: San Francisco and the Network

Phil prided himself on keeping his hands clean as he ran his very successful smuggling operation. He had more or less wandered into the business by accident. He had set out to set up a clothing goods business that would feature clothes that would appeal to women in their middle years. He had been working very hard at seeking the suppliers of the clothing goods he needed to launch the clothing line he called "The Angie Davidson Collection." It was named after his mother. He and his mother had been very close. She had been a single mother for most of their lives after his father had abandoned them. She had been a great mom who had spent every weekend taking him somewhere fun. She had kept the fun times going through his young years and later after his graduation they had still kept doing things together. Then one day, she suddenly began to feel ill. He shook his head when he thought about her rapid decline when she had been diagnosed with liver cancer.

In less than a year she had gone from a robust fun person to one who was in total misery. It had been a bitter blessing when she passed away. He had been relieved that she was no longer suffering but he was devastated. He decided to spend much of the money he had saved to do some traveling associated with starting the clothing line he wanted named after her.

The clothing line business never materialized because one evening, sitting alone in a small bar in Thailand where he had traveled to locate clothing, one of the people that he had been discussing business with and trying to arrange a shipment to the US sat down with him and asked if he was interested in making some real money by handling the shipment of goods from the US to various countries around the world.

The conversation took him by surprise, but he listened and figured out how he could actually get into the smuggling business and not immediately get arrested. He was given a Lt. Halloway's name as the person to contact. That had been the start of his now very successful smuggling operation.

He had studied the situation carefully and had hired his current staff who were mostly ignorant of what they were involved in. They thought he was in a legitimate goods distribution business. They ran the legitimate side of his business.

New Direction

He had three enforcers who he had hired from the drug trade, who were aware that they were supporting a smuggling operation. These three were happy to get out of the drug trade because his operation was safer for them and was financially as lucrative.

The smuggling business began with the connection to the Lieutenant. He kept poking around and discovered similar individuals in the Marines, Army, Air Force and National Guard. He ran all communications via a set of mailboxes. The mailboxes were the Suites of his smuggling business.

The Navy had Suite N1M.

The Army had Suite A1M.

The Air Force had Suite AF1M.

The National Guard had Suite NG1M.

All communications went through the mailboxes. He set up the Suites in five different post offices that were located around the physical office where he sat. He had the contacts give him weekly reports of what would be available and when it would be available. He in turn would give them a reply of how much the smuggled goods were worth. This worked with no hitches because he understood what each contact wanted in terms of the money he offered. He gave them more or less what they wanted.

He got the names of the interested buyers of the of the smuggled goods from his Thai contact. He sent those buyers weekly virtual bulletins of what was available with a virtual reply address. Orders for goods were taken online via an ordering Ap.

The purchase sequence was half of the money on the day of the order and the other half on the day of delivery of the goods. The buyers cleared their bank connections with the online app and once that initial connection was made the money was transferred electronically into his system.

Those wanting the smuggled goods gave the address of where the desired item was to be sent. He never took physical possession of the smuggled goods. He spent his time communicating with the suppliers and the buyers and ensuring the money for the goods showed up.

Once the money was paid he transferred that money to an account that served as the collection account. The money in this centralized account was then split. Seventy percent of it went to his business account. Twenty seven percent went to the Lieutenant or the person in the other services in a similar role to the Lieutenant and they paid those involved in their smuggling operation. Three percent was used to pay the people that worked for him in the office. He used a small portion of the seventy percent, but he did not use very much of it. He kept a low profile and was still driving his old SUV that had more than two hundred thousand miles on its odometer. He figured he would live lavishly after he "retired."

He had been surprised at the variety of items that got smuggled. He handled missiles, vehicles, quite a few torpedoes, handguns, rifles, three-, four-, six- and eight-inch cannon shells, and more recently drones had entered the picture.

All of the items were of interest to somebody in the smugglers connection. When the items came available he most often was able to immediately sell it and move it.

The smuggling operation got up and running smoothly and the money flowed in. It reminded him of the history of the California gold rush where the hard-working miners bought supplies from those providing them and never realized that not they, but the suppliers were the ones raking in the big money. In his case he was the first in what was most likely a string of reselling with each smuggler making additional huge amounts of money. He did not care. He set a price that he felt was reasonable, seldom bargained and never looked back.

In just a few years he made billions and was now contemplating getting out of the business.

Then he got wind of the Lieutenant's arrest for murder.

He thought about retirement, but he had expanded his operation and was now connected with weapons suppliers in all of the US military branches. Those connections had come about in an organic fashion. The Navy persons somehow knew someone in the Marine Corps. The Marine Corps person knew someone in the Army and the Army knew someone in the Airforce. He could not remember who had connected him to the National Guard, but they had become one of the top suppliers of goods. The connection to the Coast Guard had so far not materialized but he figured that the opportunity there was probably as blatant as with the other military branches.

He figured that he needed to make sure that all the weapons smuggled from the Navy got quickly sold. He needed to eliminate any trace of his connection with the Lieutenant's redirect of Navy goods. The connection had been a good one that had gone on for several years and had been very profitable for both of them. He knew he had made the right decision when he learned that the smuggling operation had been discovered when the Lieutenant attempted to drown a young woman who had refused his advances and then fled on the plane that had been part of the smuggling operation. He put it down to stupid moves on the Lieutenants part for both situations. He cut all communications with the Lieutenant.

He felt safe because he and his personnel had never been in the physical web of people directly handling the smuggled goods. He had provided the connections to the smugglers, and the military personnel kept the goods flowing.

He knew that getting out of the business was not as simple as saying that he quit. He needed to find someone to take over for him.

Alex and Trey had a comfortable flight to San Francisco. They were met by Linda and Lorie as they cleared the customs area.

New Direction

Linda let Alex know that Darrel, the pilot of the private jet leased by her father, would be staying and afterwards they could all fly to the Chicago Executive Airport near Evanston. She and Lorie planned a stay at their apartment there and buy a few things and get settled in before returning to Oahu.

They all drove in to the hotel in the same limo. When they arrived, Alex suggested they review how they would proceed.

Johnnie had started his on-line sleuthing at the Lieutenant's bank. He had found the link to the offshore account. Once he had hacked into the offshore bank account he was able to find the link to another offshore bank account from where the money was being sent. That account yielded several links from where the money came from. There was only one account that was linked to an account that seemed to be an account used for daily personal expenses by the person that seemed to be handling all of them. He focused on learning what he could about the individual, Phil Davidson. He found various businesses owned by the holding company Davidson ran. When he checked out the addresses of the holding companies he suspected that they were empty shell companies that might not even exist in the physical world though they had what seemed like physical addresses. He organized the information he had accumulated and sent it to Alex, Trey, Linda, and Lorie. He hoped that it was in time for them to use it. He had worked through the night, and the morning and it was now one in the afternoon which made it eleven in San Francisco.

The four of them had checked into the hotel and then gone into the restaurant and were sitting at a circular booth sipping on coffee or tea.

They were waiting for a mixed order they jokingly had called their brunch order because for some of them felt it was an early morning lunch while the others felt it was more like breakfast time when simultaneously all of their phones buzzed. They all said the same word, "Johnnie." Everyone but Alex muted their phone to prevent cross noise contamination. They listened to Johnnie explain that he had found another huge sum of offshore money that if it was seized by the IRS would be even bigger than the one that the Lieutenant had established.

He then gave them the name of the person he was sure was the distributor of the smuggled goods. He went on to share the addresses that they should check out and the address of the office of the distributor, Phil Davidson sat in. He then explained that he had Phil's customer addresses and what he thought were their bank account links but he had not had a chance to verify those connections.

Alex thanked him for his very fast work and suggested that he wait before digging into the customer information until she called him back. She suggested that he go lounge on the Golden Goose, go fishing and enjoy his time until she returned.

Lorie also thanked him and said that she really wanted to learn how he was able to get all the information so quickly. She commented that she thought the name magician did not do him justice and she thought of him as an internet wizard.

After their meal, Alex led the way to the car rental booth near the hotel lobby and rented a large black Lincoln sedan.

Lorie signed up as the second driver and accepted the keys. When they got to the car Trey and Linda got in the back seat. Lorie adjusted the seat and rear-view mirror while Alex plugged in her phone and put in the addresses in the order she wanted to visit them.

The drive to the first address took about five minutes. Lorie asked if they had the right address as she looked at the post office building from its parking lot.

Linda said she would go in and see if there was a post box with the suite number Johnnie had given them.

Trey accompanied Linda and a few minutes later they returned. They said that there was a large post office box with the letter designation that Johnnie had given them.

Alex said that she expected the next four would also be P.O. boxes, but they would verify each one.

Two hours later she declared the visits over. She suggested they drive by the last address and verify that it was an actual building. Once that was done they would call it a day and plan on arriving early the next morning and watch the arrival of the people working there.

After verifying the last address, they decided to enjoy one of the Bay area restaurants that had a view of the harbor.

After placing their orders and getting their drinks, Alex asked Linda and Lorie how they felt about the day.

Linda replied that it was somewhat of a letdown, and she had been hoping for something more concrete.

Lorie said that she too was somewhat disappointed.

Alex smiled and said that they should be feeling great. She pointed out that in just a day they had confirmed that a large part of the smuggling organization was a shell game. They had verified that the last address they would visit the following morning was a brick-and-mortar office. She declared that the goal the following day was to identify everyone that worked there and to meet Phil Davidson. She shared that Johnnie was doing a deep dig into identifying everyone that Phil communicated with. Their job was to talk to as many people as possible and learn what they knew of the operation. This was the gumshoe part of the business that usually led to a break in any case.

She shared that the following day they were all going to be playing the role of business inspectors. She would be the lead inspector and focus on the leader, the organization, and the documentation. Trey would focus on the safety issues of the environment. Linda and Lorie would interview the staff and ask what they did and about the work environment. Their goal was to find out as much as possible about the operation and what each person did.

Lorie asked what questions that she and Linda would be asking.

Alex nodded and said that after they enjoyed their meal and took a walk along the waterfront they would gather in the hotel lobby and develop a script with questions for each of them because she needed a script too.

Trey laughed and said that he certainly needed to be given a script for his safety inspection role.

Alex said that he was going to be questioning the bodyguards and should keep his cool and not be tempted to shoot any of them as he grilled them.

The meal went by quickly, and they were soon walking along the waterfront. When they got to pier thirty-nine they looked out at all the sea lions lounging on a bevy of platforms.

Lorie looked at the large number gathered on several platforms and wondered if there was a specific reason that the platforms had been provided to host the sea lions.

Trey commented that he had heard their population had greatly expanded and that they hauled out on the platforms to rest and relax. The theory was that they had been given a place to haul out near a place that had plenty of food in the nearby harbor. The platforms provided them a safe place to do so, and it kept them from trying to get into the boats. It had also become a tourist attraction, so the sea lions paid for their place to haul out.

Alex looked out at the large number of sea lions and commented that they seemed to act like a version of their human beach going counter parts, each enjoying themselves in a different way.

She then suggested they get to the hotel and develop their scripts for the following day.

Chapter 8: The Business Inspection

During the writing of the scripts, Alex realized that showing up in a black Lincoln was not the look of an inspection team. She excused herself and said that she was going to rent a plain white van. While she was doing that she called Marisa and asked her to find a sign shop in San Fransico that would be able to sell her two magnetic signs about two feet in diameter that declared that they were Business Inspectors and that she wanted to pick the signs up in the morning.

Marisa laughed and asked if this was a test of her ability to perform miracles.

Alex replied that it was not a test but that it would be great if she could get the signs.

Marisa hung up and thought for a minute and decided to contact Johnnie to see if he had any ideas.

When Johnnie answered his phone he was sitting at the kitchen table following the trails of all the contacts that Phil Davidson, the smuggler distribution king pin, had.

He laughed when Marisa explained Alex's request. He chuckled and let her know that he was used to Alex's requests. He redirected his search and soon had a sign company that boasted its ability to create any magnetic sign, at any time and have it ready in four hours. He gave that information to Marisa and suggested she call the sign shop and arrange for the signs to be available for pick up in the morning.

Marisa called the number Johnnie had given her.

The person who answered her said he could make the signs she was requesting. He asked what the two foot diameter signs should say.

Marisa replied that she wanted the signs to say, "Evercrest, McGregor, Smith and Obrien Inspectors" and it should be in Script.

The laugh she got stopped her cold. She heard the person on the other end of the phone ask if he could shorten it to "EMSO Inspectors?" If so he could get it done for five hundred per sign plus one thousand dollars for having it ready by ten in the morning.

Marisa said that would be acceptable and then asked if there might be a veterans discount.

She got another laugh and asked who the veteran was and had he seen any combat.

Marisa replied that the veteran was a Trey McGregor who had received a purple heart in Iraq. There was a moment of silence and then she was told there would be a ten percent discount if he got to meet Mr. McGregor and if he was paid in cash. Marisa said that would be no problem, got the shop owner's name, thanked him, and said that at ten sharp the next morning a white van would pull up at his shop.

She hung up and arranged for twenty-five hundred dollars in cash to be sent to the hotel where Alex was staying with instructions to give the money to her. She then called Alex and let her know about the arrangement.

Alex shared the information with the rest of the team that had just finished all of their scripts. She added that a white van would be available in the morning, and she wanted to get into position early and watch the arrival of the staff. She said that two of them would sit in the van and two of them would sit at the bus stop that was just across from the entrance to the office. She asked Linda and Lorie to be at the bus stop and take a picture of the license plate of each car entering the parking area. She would park the van so that she could get the picture of each person entering the office. At nine thirty they would all leave to get the signs for the side of the van.

"What time do we leave in the morning," Lorie asked?

"Let's plan leaving at six so we can be in place before people start arriving for work," Alex replied. She suggested they all retire to their rooms and get a good night's sleep. On the way she stopped at the desk to arrange for the van to be out front at six.

In the morning, she stopped by the desk where she was given an envelope by the receptionist. The note explained that the sign shop wanted to be paid in cash. When she got out to the van she was pleased to see that everyone else was there. She verified that they were all wearing their protective Kevlar vests. Once she had that verified she pointed at the van.

It was much nicer than she had anticipated and had bucket seats for all of them.

Trey volunteered to drive.

Lorie commented that she was not a morning person and right after they left the hotel she was snoozing.

It took about thirty minutes for them to get to their location.

Linda and Lorie got out of the van and walked about a block to the bus stop across from the office.

Alex got out her camera with a large zoom lens and adjusted the settings. She wanted license plate numbers and pictures of the drivers as they arrived. She immediately noticed that two cars were already parked. She took pictures of the cars and plates and sent them to Johnnie.

New Direction

Johnnie was set up in his office sipping on a cup of coffee when the pictures of the two cars came in. He immediately ran them through the Chicago DMV computer into which he had hacked. He learned that the older SUV was owned by Phil Davidson and the other vehicle was registered to an Ivan Lubosky who had been arrested for manslaughter, but the charge had been dropped. He sent this information out to Alex and figured that there would soon be additional license plate numbers and pictures.

Phil had arrived early to the office because he was expecting a call from one of his dealers. He had been followed from his home to the office by the three bodyguards that he had hired. He hoped to never need them, but he wanted to have the protection available and on call. He had arranged for them to have the office across from his and had one of them always standing in the hallway in front of his office. He also provided them with a Range Rover that was only two years old while he still drove his old SUV, and they had a reserved parking spot next to his car.

His support secretary rang in and let him know that the person he was meeting with was on the line. He did not pick up but instead used his phone to establish the call with that person and then hung up the landline. He was negotiating the sale of the last of the Navy armament that had arrived from Oahu. He was eager to get the set of torpedoes off his hands. He wanted to erase all connection with the Navy smuggling operation.

It was nine thirty and it seemed that everyone had arrived. Alex called Linda and Lorie back to the van. It was time for them to go get the signage for the side of their van.

When they arrived at the sign shop and went in, the owner introduced himself as Arie and asked to shake Trey's hand. He said that he had a tour of Iraq in the infantry and had been part of the initial rush across the desert at the beginning.

Trey said he was pleased to meet him and let him know that he had been in the Marines and had been a sniper. There was a moment of silence as the two stood looking at each other.

Alex inquired about the sign.

Arie smiled and said that they were done and ready to be put on the side of their van. He commented that a Marisa assured him that he would be paid in cash.

Alex smiled and said that she had the cash.

Arie picked up the two signs and walked out to the van. He expertly put the magnetic signs on, smiled, pointed at the sign, and said, "made and delivered as promised." He looked at them and said they did not seem to be inspectors, but they now had the signage that declared that they were. He led the way back into the store and handed Alex the bill for eighteen hundred dollars.

Alex looked at it and said that he deserved a tip for getting the job done as quickly as he had done it and handed him two thousand dollars in cash.

She led the way to the van and said they were off to inspect the smuggling business and see what they could learn.

When they arrived, Alex led the way in and handed the support secretary the official looking order to do the inspection. She introduced Linda and Lorie as the office inspectors, Trey as the safety inspector and herself as the leadership inspector.

The support asked for them to wait a moment

Alex watched as the support walked down the hallway to an office that had a person standing across from the door.

Phil had just gotten off the phone when there was a knock on the door. He called out, "come in."

His support explained the situation. He looked at the order to inspect. It looked official and had the embossed seal of the state Environmental Protection Agency on it. He cursed under his breath but figured the easiest way to handle the situation was to get it over with. He knew that they would find nothing out of the ordinary as part of the visit.

He got up and followed his support out to the reception area.

He looked at the four people and was somewhat apprehensive about the situation. They looked too professional and alert to be mere inspectors. He looked over his shoulder and was relieved to see his three guards standing behind him. He wondered if one of the gun runners were trying to make a move. The thought that the four might also be with law enforcement crossed his mind as well.

He introduced himself and asked why he had not been informed about the inspection.

Alex replied that the inspections were always unannounced so the inspectors would see things as they would normally be.

Phil nodded and asked how long the inspection would take.

Alex explained that it could be as short as an hour unless there were warehouses or production facilities to check. She then introduced Linda and Lorie as the office area examiners, Trey as the safety examiner and herself as the person that would interview him.

Phil nodded and invited her to come to his office. He pointed to his three guards and said that they were his safety team. He then turned and headed for his office.

Trey walked up to the three and introduced himself and asked if there was a good place where they could discuss the safety of the operation. He could tell that the three were not sure what to make of the situation. He figured he would keep asking question and get them into a discussion of their background.

Alex saw that Linda and Lorie were getting into their script. She followed Phil to his office and sat down. She first asked about his family and how everyone was.

He thanked her for asking but made the point that he had no immediate family.

It was clear to her that he was not going to be friendly about the situation.

Phil asked if she had any proof of who she was.

Alex nodded and said that she was a sherif in the San Francisco Sheriff's office and served on the inspection division during low level work periods. She pulled out her Sheriff's badge and put it on the table.

Phil's defenses went up immediately. He was impressed with the black woman's confidence, but he sensed that she was there for more than just inspecting the operation. He was right but had no idea what was really happening.

Alex planted her listening device on the underside of the desk. She knew that Johnnie would soon use it to get into the internal internet and he would be able to get into the phone system and would learn the phone numbers of all the phones.

Trey, Linda, and Lorie were planting listening devices as well.

Alex asked how long he had been in business and asked about the organizational structure.

Phil excused himself for a minute saying that he needed to get a piece of information that Alex had asked for. He went across the hall and asked for Ivan to step out for a minute. Once Ivan was out in the hall, Phil instructed him to follow the inspection van when it left to see where it went. He let him know that he was suspicious about the inspection.

He then went to the desk of his support and asked for the employees records from the beginning until now and it was to include those that had chosen to leave. He then returned to his office.

Alex had taken the time to move the listening sensor to Phil's side of the desk. The devices were smaller and thinner than a dime, were transparent and blended in with whatever background they were put on.

When he returned she was sitting where she had been when he left.

Trey watched as Ivan returned to the room. He sensed that Ivan had been given some sort of instruction. He continued asking the questions that he had prepared. It was clear to him that the three had nothing to do with safety. He noted that Ivan and Stan were buddies, and that Cheryl was the quiet one who seemed more thoughtful about her answers. She also seemed to be the person in the group that was discounted by the other two.

In just a few minutes less than an hour, Alex thanked Phil for his time and gracious consideration in how he handled the organizational review. She now had an appreciation of how cautiously Phil was handling his smuggling operation. Johnnie's information on Phil's personal record was spotless except for a couple of speeding tickets. His bodyguards were not as spotless but had not served any time in prison. She expected Lorie and Linda to find that the office help was not aware they worked in a smuggling, gun running organization because the indication was they were running a legitimate goods importing operation.

New Direction

When she walked out of Phil's office she knocked on the door across the hall and poked her head in and asked if Trey was done with his inspection. She then walked toward the entrance area and signaled Linda and Lorie as she walked out to the van. Once they were all in the van, she suggested they go for lunch and review what they had learned.

Trey stopped at the exit of the parking lot and asked where they should go for lunch. He watched as the three persons he had been interviewing walked out to the Range Rover parked by Phil's old SUV. He commented that they were most likely going to be followed.

Alex suggested they drive to the City Hall parking lot and drive in. She had her California sheriff's badge and said that would probably get them into the parking lot. Then once they were in the parking lot they could check to see if their tail left. Once that was accomplished, she suggested they go to the waterfront and enjoy a leisurely lunch.

Ron Mueller

Chapter 9: Retaliation

Johnnie spent the entire day sorting through the various phone connections. From those connections, he determined that the office workers were just that. They were making daily calls to legitimate goods import companies, handling the daily calls, paying daily bills, or logging in payments to banks. Their calls had no connection with any of the smugglers that called in.

He learned that the bodyguards were just that as well and spent a great deal of time chatting with friends about how great of a job they had as compared with their time in the drug trade.

He was impressed how Phil kept his legitimate business well documented, very legally run with taxes paid and it was disconnected from the smuggling operation. His legal import business focused on finding and importing any goods that was popular with the general public. He was making enough to pay his workers, give them good benefits and still make enough to put a large profit in the bank. He would have been a high-end multi-millionaire from his legitimate business.

He was as well very impressed on how carefully Phil managed his illegitimate business. He was making a huge profit on the goods that he accepted from the Navy, Army, Air Force and National Guard. The fact that his smuggling empire included these armed forces surprised Johnnie. He found the volume of stolen military hardware unbelievable. He was not surprised to find huge sums of money in offshore bank accounts. The accounts were kept separate and designated to indicate with which armed force it was associated. There were several billion dollars in each account. It was a huge sum of money that was earning Phil a phenomenal amount by being invested in the stock market. The money was all untaxed and would be seized by the IRS as soon as they found out about it.

He organized the accounts so that the IRS could seize each of them separately. There was a fifth account that was just in Phil's name that had close to three billion dollars in it. This account was most likely half illegitimate and half legitimate. It was kept in investments that spanned the financial investment market offering. This account would take the IRS more work to determine how much of it was legitimate and had taxes paid on the legitimate money. Johnnie figured that would be their problem.

New Direction

During the time Johnnie was digging out all the financial information, Phil was busy trying to figure out who had visited his office. He was sure that more than "inspecting" the safe operation of his business had been underway. He had his folks look for any bugs, but none were found.

When his bodyguards returned and informed him that the van that they had followed had entered the main city office building parking lot, he put in a call to the informant that he had there. She called back and let him know that no business safety inspection had been scheduled for his business and in fact that organization was so far behind they only inspected those businesses where a major accident or death had taken place. She added that there was no Alex Evercrest listed as an employee in any of the San Francisco City organizations.

This information triggered Phil to ask his secretary to check all San Francisco hotels to see if she could find an Alex Evercrest registered in any of them.

Almost by accident Johnnie ran back through all the phone taps that he had set up and was surprised when he discovered that the office support secretary was checking the registration of hotels for Alex. He decided to continue monitoring and was listening when the hotel that Alex and the rest were staying in verified that they had a guest with that name. He immediately put in a call to Alex.

Johnnie's ring let Alex know who was calling. The four of them were sitting in an almost deserted outdoor area of the restaurant in a corner where the rain torrent, which had started when they got there, was not bothering them. She put her phone on speaker mode and set it on the center of the table.

Johnnie began with, "You have all been made." He then explained that he had overheard Phil's support secretary searching hotels for them and was listening when she learned the hotel where they were staying.

Alex thanked him for the heads up and let him know that she and the team would handle the situation.

Johnnie then added that he had found and documented all the offshore bank accounts and had the dollar value for each. He added that there was over ten billion dollars sitting out in those accounts.

Alex thanked him for the good news and asked him to contact Joe Brown and find out who the IRS contact would be that would handle the five offshore accounts and let her know as soon as possible.

Johnnie ended the conversation by wishing them a safe return to their hotel.

Alex looked around the table and then at the rain that seemed to be giving its all to get to them.

She looked at Trey and said that they would need to be super cautious when they returned to the hotel. She added that she would like Linda and Lorie to take the lead when they returned to the hotel and go into the reception area and make sure that there was no one there that they had seen at the business. She would drop them off one block from the hotel and they should walk casually in. She and Trey would drive past the hotel and Trey would walk back and go in next. She would drive into the entrance area and come in last.

The rain seemed to cooperate and stop as they got ready to leave the restaurant. Alex asked that they take off the signs on the side of the van and put them in the carrying case. She laughed and said that they now had their signs for their next unsuccessful try at being elusive sleuths.

Lorie asked what they should do once they were in the lobby.

Alex suggested they go to the area where the internet café was set up and pretend to use one of the computers. If any of the three bodyguards were present they should be ready to protect themselves. She added that she did not think they would be there otherwise their entrance sequence would be the other way around.

As they turned into the street of the hotel entrance, the older SUV parked in front of the dark green Range Rover stood out like a sore thumb to Alex.

She asked Trey what he saw.

He replied that some inexperienced group of people interested in finding them were parked along the street leading to the hotel.

As they went by he added that they all seemed to be in the vehicles.

Alex said that there was a change in their plan. They would all go in at the same time. She asked that the three get out on the hotel entrance side of the van and she would get out of the driver's side and walk quickly around after they had made it through the front door.

She asked Trey to secure the inside area and that once she got in he should keep an eye out for Phil and his bodyguards. She was going to go directly to the elevator and go to the top floor to her suite. He, Linda, and Lorie should come up after a few minutes. She let him know that the "shave and a haircut knock" was his safe entry signal.

Trey replied that he had her back, and he would be up to make sure they had the firepower to face whatever might happen.

When they got to the drop off circle he led the way in and immediately positioned himself so he could see past the van to the sidewalk.

Once they got in, Linda walked over to the elevators and got one ready for Alex to use.

Alex got out of the van, let the valet know that she was keeping the keys and would shortly return and then she walked past Trey got into the elevator and Linda joined her.

Once she was in the elevator Trey waited for three minutes and then sent Lorie to get an elevator and hold it for them. He continued to watch. Then he turned and walked briskly across the lobby and got into the elevator with Lorie.

Once they got to Alex's hotel room door, Lorie laughed when Trey gave the "shave and a haircut knock," and was let in.

She commented that she had looked over her shoulder to see if Al Capone and his gunmen were behind them in the hallway, but it was clear.

Alex gave Linda and Lorie each a pillow and said that their role was to throw the pillows at whoever came through the door and then fall to the floor. She went on to say that she and Trey would be the ones doing the shooting if it was necessary.

Phil was sitting in his SUV thinking about what he was going to do. He figured that his smuggling business was at risk, and he needed to do something forceful. He needed to eliminate whoever was trying to either take over his business or trying to close it down. Either way, he was going to have his three bodyguards earn their pay and eliminate all four of the people that had dared to come to his office to snoop around.

He would start with the person who had interviewed him. He would kill her, then go to each of the other rooms and kill each of them. He instructed his three bodyguards to use silencers and to shoot on sight.

He had a universal key card for the hotel that would get them in without the need to knock. He led the way toward the hotel. He noted that the van no longer had any signage on it, but he had observed the young black woman get out of the driver's side and was sure she would be in her room. The lack of the signs gave him confidence that he was doing the right thing.

He was sure he would surprise her. He led the way to the elevators as he waved at the receptionist. He punched the button for the top floor. He wondered what business his first target was in that she could afford to get one of the best rooms in the hotel.

He led the way down the hallway to the room. He handed the key card to Ivan and then stood to the side.

Ivan quietly slid the key card in the lock and then gun in hand he pushed the door open. He was hit in the face by a pillow and reactively fired toward the person that had thrown it. His gun never made it back to Alex who was standing in front of him. The last thing he saw was the gun dropping from his hand and the world going black. His knees buckled and he fell face first to the floor.

Stan, who was standing behind him, raised his gun as Ivan fell to his knees in front of him. He too was surprised by two holes in his chest and the fact that the world was slowly turning dark.

New Direction

Cheryl did not hesitate she dropped her weapon and ran down the hallway towards the elevators. She could hear Phil running at her heals. She pressed the down button and was relieved that the elevator doors opened immediately. She rushed in with Phil behind her and pressed one. The ride down seemed to take forever and when the doors opened she ran across the lobby and out the door.

Phil caught up with her and suggested they take his SUV and go directly to the private airfield where he kept his plane. She ran to the Range Rover, retrieved a rifle and her purse. Once in the car she asked the name of the person who had been doing the shooting. When she heard the name she let out a groan and commented that they were both in deep do da because they had just attacked the most successful detective in the country.

Phil asked her about what she was talking.

She replied that Alex Evercrest was a dead shot, had hunted down the worst criminals in the country and was known for always getting the person she chased. She added that they could run but eventually they would be caught. She shook her head and said that it was their death day.

When they got to the airfield, Cheryl said that she was not going with him but was going to stay and walk away into the sun set. She had enough money to tide her over until she could get some low paying job and get a new identity. She wished Phil good luck and started to walk away.

He laughed and said that he had enough money tucked away that he would go to some island in the Pacific and live a life of luxury. He offered Cheryl a ride in comfort to a place of paradise.

Cheryl shook her head, turned to walk away.

Phil stopped her and said that he had her severance pay. He said he had twenty thousand dollars for her as her severance pay. He went to the back of his SUV and gave her a briefcase and wished her good luck.

She thanked him, wished him good luck, turned, walked away, and waved her hand over her head. She had left the rifle in the back of the SUV. She walked back towards the highway.

Phil shook his head and got his plane ready for takeoff. He made sure he had enough fuel to get to Hawaii.

Back at the hotel, Alex called in the shooting. She took a picture of the gun in the hallway, marked the spot where it was dropped, carried it back into the apartment and placed it on the sink countertop. She put her weapon there as well.

It took the local police about five minutes to show up.

During that time, she put in a call to Jane Stradford, her Illinois Lieutenant Governor boss, and quickly explained the situation.

Jane let her know that she would call the Police Chief in San Francisco and clear the way for her.

Alex then called Harold Zimmerman, the Chicago DEA head and her personal friend and let him know about the situation and the fact that she had uncovered a very successful gun runner.

He let her know that he would alert the San Francisco DEA to get involved in the case and that he would most likely get to her hotel while the police were still there.

When the police arrived, Alex showed them her California sheriffs badge and briefly explained the scene. She pointed to her weapon that she had put on the counter next to a gun dropped by one of the attackers who had run away and said that it was the only gun that had been fired.

The policeman in charge asked why no one else had done any shooting.

Trey commented that Alex was exceedingly fast and had never hesitated when the two attackers barged in and started to shoot.

Alex shook her head and replied that there was no one else to shoot at for the other three but their weapons were all properly registered in the state of California.

The coroner arrived and commented on the accuracy of each shot. He asked where she had learned to shoot.

Alex smiled and said that she spent four hours each week at the practice range.

When he heard her name, he shook his head and said that he had watched a recruiting movie at a police convention that featured her. He asked why the two gunmen were after her.

She replied that she was after their boss who had successfully fled the scene with a third potential shooter who had dropped her weapon and run.

She had just finished answering when Audrey Wilson walked in and introduced himself as the San Francisco DEA and asked about the person who she was pursuing.

Immediately after his introduction, the San Francisco Chief of Police, Reily Hinderland, walked in and introduced himself. He commented that he had been asked by his boss to help her out. He looked around and said that it did not seem she needed his protection, but he needed to know more about what led to the shooting.

Alex asked him to sit down, and she would explain to him and Audrey about a large-scale smuggling ring that a Phil Davidson was running. And about the two gunmen that worked for him who she had shot and killed.

Chapter: 10 Out of the Frying Pan into the Fire

Phil taxied out on the runway for takeoff. He had put in a flight plan to go to Vancouver but planned to revise it once he was in the air when he changed control towers. He figured that would make it harder for anyone trying to figure out where he was going to keep track. He figured that at least in the short term it would give him some breathing room.

Johnnie was tracking Phil's phone and was able to get his position while he was still close to the California coast. He kept a close eye on the direction and when it seemed fixed and just before he lost the phone contact he had the direction figured out. He knew that Phil was headed toward Hawaii. He was not sure which island but once Phil got close enough to be within range of the Hawaiian phone towers, he would be able to locate him again. He called Alex and let her know where Phil was headed.

Alex laughed and said that she was looking forward to going there as well. She asked Johnnie to lock down all of Phil's financial accounts so he would be denied access to his money.

Once she was off the phone, she looked over at Linda and Lorie who were sitting on the couch chatting with the police Chief and the DEA rep and asked if Darrel was willing to fly them back to Hawaii.

Linda asked if that was where Phil was headed.

Alex nodded and said she was not sure which island, but they could start out with Maui as the goal and adjust if they found out it was some other island.

Lorie laughed and said that Phil was headed toward their favorite location in the world. He should get a break when he was charged with smuggling.

The police Chief said that she would get her weapon back once it was processed and no longer needed.

Audry added that he would work with Reily and determine what the DEA would do about the smuggling operation.

Phil put his plane on auto pilot. The time to get to Maui was about five hours so he decided to take a nap and figure out what he would do once he got there. He knew he would continue across the pacific, but he wanted to take a break on Maui and get things organized and enjoy the weather while he was there. His house faced west and was on the other side of the road from the LOLO cove. He loved the location and had his house always ready for an impromptu visit. He would go there, decompress and plan what he would do next. He was confident that he had made a clean getaway and had at least a few days on his side.

New Direction

He figured after a brief stay on the island he would fly on to either Osaka, Japan, or Manila in the Philippines. He had a condo in Osaka and usually stayed at the Manila Hotel in the Philippines. He figured that if the hotel was good enough for General MacArthur and his family, it was good enough for him. He was leaning toward Manila because the Philippines had more lenient entry requirements as compared to Japan.

Alex and the rest made it to the airport where they were met by Darrel and led to the plane. Once they were all on board he said that he would fly at max speed, and they should get to Maui close to the time that Phil would get to Hawaii. He added that he would change the destination if they learned which island Phil was headed for. He suggested they all relax, enjoy the refreshments and he would do the hard work of sitting in the cockpit.

Lorie laughed and said that she felt sorry for the huge exertion and strain that he would experience and asked if she should hold his hand.

He said that he would enjoy her holding his hand and he was certain it would reduce the strain he would feel.

Alex said that she was going to take a nap and suggested they all do the same.

Linda called her mother and let her know that she, Lorie, Alex, and Trey were all flying to Maui. She filled her in on the fact that they were in pursuit of a smuggler that was headed towards Hawaii.

Brian came on the line and asked for additional information such as the name and type of airplane they were pursuing.

Linda gave him Phil's name but said she had no idea what type of plane he was flying. She said that he should check in with Johnnie since he was doing the on-line tracking of Phil.

Brian replied that he would do a little digging to see if he could find out which island Phil was flying into.

Even as Brian was beginning his search for flight information, Johnnie was checking on home ownership on the Islands. He broke down laughing when he found the address of the house registered under Phil's name.

Mary asked him what he was laughing about.

He let her know that Alex was in pursuit of a smuggler who had escaped from San Francisco and was flying to the Hawaiian Islands where he had a house less than a mile from her waterfront house.

Mary started laughing as well.

He sent a text message with the address to Alex and wished he could be there when she received it.

He had no sooner sent the message than he got a call from Brian asking what he might have on Phil.

Johnnie shared that address and asked if Brian knew his neighbor.

Brian and Kekoa were sitting together, and both started laughing when they saw the address.

Kekoa made the point that Phil was Alex's next-door neighbor not theirs.

Johnnie shared the fact that he had locked Phil out of access to his bank accounts so money might be a problem for him.

Kekoa said that was great but pointed out that, if Phil was a seasoned smuggler, he most likely had emergency funds stashed away, and he likely had contacts on the Islands that could provide him with additional funding if needed.

A few hours later, as they got close to the island, Alex's phone registered the text message from Johnnie.

She started laughing and read the message out loud.

That had everyone on the plane laughing.

Lorie commented that it was the case of jumping out of the frying pan and into the fire.

When Phil landed he taxied to the private jet parking area where he tied down his plane. He had it serviced for gas and had the engine checked. Once he had the plane ready for takeoff, he took a cab to his beachside home. He relaxed on the drive across the island and stopped at one of his favorite restaurants and had his evening meal. He enjoyed the house special for dinner and had a glass of wine to go along with it.

During his meal he pondered his situation. He was worried about how he was going to handle his business. He figured he should check in with his staff to see if they were still in operation. If so he would contact his network of gun runners and make sure that the equipment and armament they were interested in was made available. The Navy link was dead, but the other connections were still operational.

When the taxi taking him to his home on Makena Road passed the fourth police car, his radar was on full alert. He asked the taxi driver to take him all the way past Ahihi Cove and then turn around in the parking lot before the continuous lava fields.

He counted three additional police cars just past his house. He decided that somehow they had figured out where he was going.

He told the cab driver that there was a change in plans and to take him back to the airport.

It was definitely time to continue his journey. He would stop at the big island where he had a stash of money, passports and two handguns. He had seen his top two gunmen go down, so he knew that this detective that was after him was not shy about shooting.

Once he landed on the big island he immediately had his gas tank topped off and the plane serviced.

When he continued, he would fly at about three quarters speed to ensure that he would have plenty of gas to get to Manila.

New Direction

He went to the edge of the field in front of the plane where an old storage shed was standing and opened the lock. He went to the chest that was up against the far wall. He opened it and picked up the satchel that held one hundred and fifty thousand dollars. An old leather briefcase had a set of passports, two revolvers and some clips that held extra ammunition. He picked them up and carried them back to the plane.

He took a moment and went over to the vending machines where he purchased several bags of chips, two candy bars and three soft drinks. He returned to his plane and put in a flight plan to Oahu.

He had decided to fly to Manila but would put in a second flight plan later or not at all.

Back on Maui, Darrel brought the plane in for a smooth landing and taxied over to the hanger where he kept the plane. He helped everyone off and pointed to a black van that was parked near the entrance.

Annie and Brian were walking towards them. They all shared hugs and then Brian said that he had the police out trying to apprehend Phil but so far they had not been able to do so.

Alex thanked him and let him know that Johnnie had tracked Phil to Maui and then had tracked him to the big island where he stayed for a little over an hour. He was now heading across the Pacific towards the Philippines. She added that what she would like to do was to get a search warrant to search his house to see if she could find something that would give her a clue where in the Philippines he was going.

Brian made a call and afterwards said that they could drive to Phil's house and a search warrant would be there when they arrived.

During the search of the house, Linda kept commenting on what a great place it was and how she would love to have a place like it.

Lorie held up a brochure featuring the Manila Hotel.

Alex said they were through with the search of the house and should plan on getting on the plane and heading for Manila.

Trey said he was game, but he reminded everyone that they had a dinner invitation that evening.

Linda said that she would let Darryl know that they wanted to take off bright and early the next morning.

Lorie nodded and said that she was not going to miss dinner at her favorite restaurant.

New Direction

While the dinner on Maui was being enjoyed, Phil landed in Manila and after having his plane serviced and tied down, he headed to one of his favorite local restaurants for a decent meal. He planned to enjoy it and then check in to the Manila Hotel, take a shower and enjoy a good night's sleep. He had concluded that running to escape was exhausting.

The next morning, after breakfast, he tried to access his primary offshore account. He was surprised that he was not able to do so. He sequentially tried the other five accounts only to learn that he was locked out of them as well. He wondered who had the power to do such a thing. He figured he would be able to get them reinstated if he went to each bank in person. He figured he would do so after he had made sure he had made his escape. In the short term he had one hundred and fifty thousand dollars to tide him over.

He spent the afternoon contacting his customers and arranging deliveries of weapons and other materials in which they were interested. He went to a bank that was walking distance from the hotel and opened an account and asked his customers to send the money there. He put five thousand dollars into the account and also rented a security box where he put one hundred forty thousand and his extra pistol.

The next thing he wanted to do was to find a place outside of the downtown Manila area where he could set up a more permanent residence

The next morning when Alex and the rest of the team arrived at the Maui airport and met Darryl. He asked how fast they wanted to get to Manila and stated that if they wanted the top speed, he would need to put his long-distance extra fuel tank in the luggage compartment, if he flew at his normal cruise speed, he would not need the extra fuel.

Alex said that his normal cruise speed would be fine. She added that she was more interested in getting to Manila safely.

Once they were all on board, Alex got on the phone and talked with Johnnie. She asked him to verify the arrival of Phil to the Manila Hotel and see if he could find out the room number.

Johnnie felt good about his involvement in the chase. He also felt good about his involvement in identifying the rest of the smuggling network participants. He was sure that his "follow the money trail" was going to pay off as well. What he felt best about the whole thing was that in the past week he had gone out on the Golden Goose fishing twice, had caught several bass and had slept in his own bed every night.

Alex's second call was to Joe Brown to verify the IRS agents that would be involved. She let Joe know that she was interested in Phil's Maui home and his airplane as part of the finder's reward. She figured it was better to ask early.

Joe said that it he was sure both the IRS and the various military financial people that would be involved would rather reward her with physical property since that was always harder to handle.

New Direction

The final call was to Matt to let him know where she was going and to see when it would be a good time to call so she could talk to Aurea.

Matt laughed and said any time other than three in the morning.

Chapter 11: End of the Line

Phil woke up, left the hotel for the airport, and flew north to Laoag to look at several places along the Padsan River. He had previously looked at places there and knew a realtor there that he contacted. He found the place he wanted and put down enough money to hold it, but he realized he would need to get his accounts unfrozen if he wanted to close the deal. He would try once again to access his other accounts, but he figured he could easily redirect the flow of any new payments to his new bank account, and he would have the money he needed in just a few weeks. This realization put him at ease, and he felt that he was going to be successful in his getaway.

He flew back to Manila where he once again had his plane fueled and prepped. He then took a taxi to a restaurant near the Manila Hotel. He went in, ordered, and enjoyed a nice traditional lunch of Seafood Adobo. His lunch was one of the best he had recently eaten. He took the time to call his customers, went for a leisurely walk in the park on his way back to his Manila Hotel room.

Everything was going as planned and he felt good about his escape.

Suddenly he realized that the tall white guy with a green ball cap ahead of him was the same guy that had been part of the fake security inspection of his office back in San Francisco.

Immediately afterwards he spotted the black female who had interviewed him walking about ten feet ahead of the green ball cap guy.

He figured the two young females following a little farther behind were part of the group.

He paused for a moment and made sure his weapon was fully loaded. He now wished he had the second pistol he had put in the safety deposit box. He grabbed a full clip with his left hand and stepped into the bushes.

He took aim at the center of the black female's back and fired twice. He then immediately shot the tall guy twice in the back. His next four shots were for the two women. One of them had turned and got shot in the chest the other got shot in the back.

He then turned and ran away keeping the bushes between him and the four he had just shot. He almost knocked over a young mother pushing her baby carriage. He knew he needed to get back to his plane and once again figure out how to get away.

New Direction

Alex staggered forward when the bullets hit her in her back. She turned to shoot but did not see her target. She hesitated to shoot at all because the park was full of young women and children. She saw that Trey had been hit as well, like her, he had turned to return fire but did not. She looked over to where Linda and Lorie were checking on each other.

She had not expected to be ambushed in the middle of the busy park. She hesitated only a moment and then put in a call to Darrel and asked him to keep Phil from being able to take off in his plane and that she and the rest of the team were on the way over.

Alex was surprised that the shooting seemed to have gone unnoticed or at least ignored by the people in the park. She checked with Trey, Linda, and Lorie to see if anyone was going to have more than bruises.

Lorie replied that she was really upset at getting shot without a chance of shooting back. She complained that the last time she was shot, her ribs hurt for a week. Now she was going to have a pain in her back for the next two weeks and her suit jacket and blouse had multiple holes through them.

Linda added that she now knew what it felt like to be shot, and it was worse than the proverbial kick of a mule. She had been shot once in the back and had turned only to get hit in the chest.

Trey said that he had gone through getting shot enough times that he was focused on getting even and wanted to get to Phils plane.

Alex put in a call to Darrel and asked him to make sure that Phil could not take off in his plane.

Then she hailed a taxi and asked the driver to get to the airport as fast as possible.

Darrel had let Alex know that he would make sure that Phil would not be able to take off. He walked over to where Phil's jet was tied down and checked that the tie downs were designed to be locked. He walked back to his plane and opened his toolbox, took out two locks, walked back to Phil's jet and put the locks on the cables attached to the wings.

He then walked back to his jet, locked everything up and went into the hangar's snack room and bought a bag of chips and a soft drink. He had been about to go to lunch but now figured he would wait for Alex and the rest of them to get to the hangar. He called Alex back and let her know that Phil would not be taking off in his plane.

Phil walked briskly to the edge of the park to a cab that was parked in the shade of a large banyan tree. He got in, asked the driver to drive to the hotel and wait a moment while he went to get his suitcase.

He had expected the police to show up, but the park seemed quiet.

He figured the four he had shot were either dead or critically wounded but he made sure that the four were nowhere in sight and then walked briskly to the elevator and took it up to his floor. He entered his room and hurriedly packed his bag. He looked around to make sure he was not leaving anything that would give away where he was going. He pulled his bag to the elevator, went down, and returned to the waiting cab. His current plan was to fly to Laoag and stay in the condo that he had agreed to lease.

He then asked the driver to take him to the airport where the private planes parked. He tried to relax during the thirty-minute drive but kept looking behind the taxi to make sure no one was following.

While Phil was getting prepared to leave, Alex flagged down a cab and the four of them left immediately for the airport. When they arrived, she thanked the taxi driver for a very exciting ride and gave him a big tip.

She saw that Phil's plane was still there and Phil was not in sight. They all walked into the hanger area and over to the snack room.

Darrel stood up and said that he was glad to see them and added that he thought they had arrived before Phil because he expected Phil to come in and go to the office to ask why his plane was locked down.

Alex thanked Darrel, turned, and asked Linda and Lorie if they were feeling up to confronting Phil.

Lorie asked if it was OK for her to shoot him.

Alex laughed, shook her head, and said that they would first try to arrest him and only resort to any shooting if he pulled a weapon.

Phil looked out of the taxi as it arrived at the private plane hangar. He paid the driver and gave him a tip for having waited and wished him a good day. He then pulled his bag over to where his plane was parked. He took his bag into the plane and decided that he would fire it up and get the air conditioning going to cool down the interior. He then went out to release the tie downs. When he got to the wing tie downs he realized that they were locked on. He wondered why that had been done.

He looked around suspiciously but saw no one. He reentered the plane, got his gun, and put the extra clips into his pocket. He then headed for the hangar to see who had the keys to the locks. He walked into the main office and asked about the tie down locks.

The young female clerk asked him to wait for a moment. She turned and asked two young men in blue coveralls who were sitting and chatting if they had locked down the plane in question.

Both of them shook their heads in the negative and said that they had not locked down any planes.

In his frustration, Phil pulled his gun and said that he did not care who had locked down the plane, but they should get a bolt cutter and cut the locks off because he was ready to leave.

New Direction

The two stood up and held up their hands and said he should follow them out to where the tools were, and they would go and cut off the locks.

Phil put his gun back into his pocket and followed the two out of the back door of the office.

Alex saw Phil exiting from the office and she quietly said they should leave the snack room and spread out. They would follow the three out to the plane and see if they could surprise Phil and get the upper hand. She reminded everyone that she would do the talking and if necessary the initial shooting.

Phil followed the two hanger personnel out to his plane. They walked over to the far wing cable and cut the lock off.

He was following them around to the wing near the planes entrance door when he realized that the four people he had shot and thought he had killed were spread out in front of him.

He told the two mechanics to stop. He stood behind them and called out that he was getting on the plane and leaving. He said that he would shoot each of the mechanics if anyone tried to stop him. He guided the two mechanics over to the wing and told the one holding the bolt cutter to cut the lock.

After the cable fell to the ground, Phil looked to where the four were standing and realized that each of them was pointing their weapon towards him. He was fully shielded by the two mechanics and decided that he should shoot the four before they knew what he was doing.

He raised his weapon slightly and was ready to shoot the black female first when magically he watched his gun fall out of his hand as his world went dark.

Alex had been closely watching Phil, when she saw him glance her way and begin to point his gun her way, she fired one shot. She watched the gun fall from Phil's hand as a small hole appeared just above his nose and began to bleed.

She watched as Phil's knees seemed to buckle as he fell forwards. He landed in a prone position as if he was bowing to her. It reminded her of the first person who she had shot and killed who ended up in the same position.

The two mechanics bolted away as Phil fell limply to the ground. Once they got past the four, they both stopped to look back.

Trey walked over to where Phil was now lying face down and then looked at Alex and said that once again she had not given anyone else a chance to shoot.

Alex asked the two mechanics to call the police.

She called Captain Kirpatrick back in San Diego, explained what had happened and asked him if he knew anyone in the Navy stationed in Manila that might be able to give her a hand.

The Captain said that he knew several of the brass there and he would give them a call. He asked where they could get in touch with her.

She said that she would most likely be sitting in a police station trying to explain the situation to the local police, but they could get in touch with her on her phone.

She turned and suggested that Darrel take everyone for a flight along the coast and return after a couple of hours. She would stay and handle the local police.

Linda spoke up and said that she was not going anywhere. They had all been shot at, they had all been ready to shoot again and she was not worried about the local police.

Trey smiled and said that she knew better than to suggest he leave.

Lorie laughed and said that the only thing she was mad about was that she was not the one who had shot Phil and that she wanted to finish this up, enjoy a traditional Philippine dinner and go out shopping for new clothes.

The police seemed to arrive in mass. They asked what had happened and who shot the person on the ground.

Alex became the spokesperson for the group as she handed her gun to the officer. She explained that Phil had been fleeing from the US as he tried to avoid arrest for smuggling. She described his flight to Hawaii and then his escape from there and his flight to the Philippines. She shared the fact that she and her team followed him and that he had ambushed them at the park near the Manila Hotel.

She then explained he was in the process of trying once again to escaped via his plane. She pointed to the two mechanics and said that their lives had been threatened and when Phil raised his gun to shoot, she had shot and killed him before he could shoot anyone else.

One of the mechanics said something in Tagalog and the police looked over at Alex and asked her how she had been able to shoot and miss the two mechanics.

Alex smiled and said there was an inch between their two heads, so she had plenty of room.

The policeman said that he now understood why the two mechanics kept talking about the fact that they thought they were going to die but that a miracle had happened. He added that the miracle was that she was an excellent shot.

Alex nodded and said that she would not have taken the shot if she thought she would miss.

The policeman took a call, looked at Alex and said that he had been instructed to take her to the main police station for a debriefing.

The ride to the station took about thirty minutes. They arrived and were met at the curb by two Navy officers. One was a captain and the second was a lieutenant. The captain said that he had been asked to help her in any manner that she needed.

Alex thanked him and said that she just needed to make sure that the local police knew she was on a legitimate chase of a dangerous criminal that had been running a smuggling ring. She had registered her teams weapons as required by the Philippine government and had entered with all the proper paperwork. She just wanted to make sure the local police did not overreact because she had killed the person she had been chasing.

The Captain let her know that he had been informed by his friend in San Diego of the situation. He had contacted the head of the police department and had set up a meeting with him.

Alex thanked him. She looked at Trey, Linda, and Lorie and asked them if they were ready for the meeting.

Trey said that he would like a moment to call home then he was set.

Linda and Lorie made a similar request.

Alex smiled and said she had a couple of calls to make as well.

They all walked over into that shade of a large tree and stood making their calls.

Her first call was to Johnnie. She asked him to get everything wrapped up and ready for the IRS. She let him know that she wanted the jet plane and the house.

Johnnie said that he had already been in contact with the IRS, and they had indicated that they were quite happy to grant her all the physical assets that Phil owned that was associated with the smuggling. They had also let him know that they would only be getting a fifteen percent finders reward because the military branches wanted the money to make up for their smuggling losses.

Alex laughed and said that fifteen percent of twelve billion was how much?

She asked if he was going to be satisfied with his two hundred and twenty-five million before taxes share or was he going to fight for a higher percentage.

Johnnie laughed and said that he had gone from sleeping under Cincinnati over passes to now worrying about how much tax he was paying for a fortune. He said that he would be happy for just another tray of her cookies.

Alex agreed to bake the cookies once she was back in Evanston.

After hanging up she called Matt, who asked what was wrong. She responded that everything was fine.

He asked if she realized that once again it was three in the morning.

Alex apologized and quickly explained what had happened and that she was just calling to let him know she was OK and that she loved him.

Matt thanked her for calling. He said that in the morning he would let Aurea, and the rest of the family know what had happened.

Alex hung up, looked around to find everyone ready to go in and talk with the police.

Ron Mueller

Chapter: 12 Celebration

The discussion at the police station lasted about two hours. Alex was pleased with the help she got from the Navy Captain and Lieutenant and invited them out to dinner. They both thanked her but declined because they both had their family to get home to.

Alex suggested they all go out shopping first and have dinner at the usual late starting time that was the habit in the Philippines.

The shopping turned out to be a great way to decompress from the tension of the day. Each of them was able to find several new outfits.

Trey said he was having his new outfit tailor fit and adjusted and he was happy to find the variety of hats that fit him. He said that he had bought several hats for Matt, her father and Mother, Johnnie, and Mary.

Alex, After finding a replacement outfit for herself she bought several outfits for Aurea.

Linda and Lorie both said that they had found several outfits that they like and would be going home and enjoying them,

At dinner Alex got a call from Johnnie letting her know that he had expedited the transfer of ownership of the plane and the house on Maui. He had also accepted the office building in San Francisco and a yacht that was anchored in Maui. He said that he hoped that his decision to accept the physical items as part of the reward was acceptable.

Alex let him know that she thought he was doing a great job interfacing with the IRS and would make sure to reward him with several trays of cookies. She heard Mary comment that Johnnie didn't need fattening up.

She then asked Johnnie to find a pilot qualified to fly the companies new jet plane. They also needed to rent a spot at the Executive Airport where they could keep it.

She hung up and let Linda and Lorie know about the house and yacht in Maui.

Linda came over and gave her a hug and said that she was looking forward to being her Maui neighbor.

Lorie commented that they would probably take the yacht to Oahu where they could use it on weekends when they were there.

She then called Matt and was able to speak to him, Aurea, and her mother. She let them know that she was returning late the following day.

She then made plans with Trey, Linda, and Lorie to all go back to Evanston so they could have an official business meeting. She wanted to review all the packages going to the IRS and to see what loose ends needed to be closed as part of the case.

She worked with the Navy captain to handle Phil's body and get it returned to California.

Darrel let them know that the shortest flight back was through Portland where he would need to refuel before they flew on to Illinois.

Alex commented that she planned to catch up on her sleep on their way back and she hoped that the pain in her back would subside.

The flight back was long but uneventful. They landed and agreed that the next day they would all meet at the office at ten.

Alex took a taxi home and had a surge of fond memories as the taxi drove through the tunnel made by the tree branches over the driveway. When Aurea came running out to greet her she felt a surge of love and jumped out to give her a hug. She took a moment to pay the taxi driver and then picked Aurea up and carried her toward the front door.

Matt came out and gave her a hug and Aurea got down and took her hand and said that everyone was out by the pool.

Alex was happy that everyone was only her parents and Johnnie and Mary. She got hugs from everyone and led to the table that had a variety of food. She looked down the table at three meat offerings. There was prime rib roast, coconut shrimp and a simple pan-fried trout as the choice of meats. She also saw that there was a dish of sliced tomatoes with vinegar, olive oil and parsley which was one of her favorites. She decided on a thin slice of prime rib and a few slices of tomato.

After she had her plate she took it over where everyone was sitting and asked Johnnie how his work with the IRS was going.

He smiled and said that he had been able to get them to up their reward percentage to twenty percent and he had been able to get the deeds to the physical parts of the reward.

Alex said that she would bake a couple of trays of cookies so the team would have them for their ten o'clock in the morning meeting.

Matt let her know that the Golden Goose was now being rented out three days a week. He was reserving Saturdays for going out fishing with Aurea, but they preferred going out on the Minnow, so the Golden Goose was going out on Saturdays with Dexter as the captain. So far he had kept Sundays open for family use.

Alex asked how the construction of the restaurant was going.

Her mother spoke up and said that the kitchen was done and scheduled for a trial. She added that she was going to cook their dinner after the Golden Goose came in from fishing on Sunday. The fish would be cleaned in the special kitchen cleaning station and prepared for roasting in the oven, deep fried and grilled. She commented that this would let her test the ovens, the grill, and the deep fryer. She would also serve a lamp chop for each person. Her new chef and three waiters and waitresses would serve all of them on the newly completed indoor section of the restaurant.

New Direction

Alex said that she would make Sunday's fishing a celebration of a very successful start to the two new businesses. She figured that between the two businesses she would have twelve people participating in the celebration.

Rose-Anne said that was a great idea and she would make sure there was enough of everything.

Johnnie let her know that he had found a pilot for her jet that lived locally that she might want to invite to verify that he was the person she would want as a permanent hire.

Alex asked Aurea to bring her the small blue suitcase that had a bow on the handle.

Aurea rushed out and came back with the bag.

Alex unzipped it and took out two dresses, some black slacks and three blouses, and a black suit outfit.

Aurea looked at each and excitedly said she was going to try them on and see how they fit.

During the time she was doing that, Trey went and got the hats that he had brought as gifts and gave them to Russel, Johnnie, Matt, Rose-Anne, and Mary.

Rose-Anne gave him a hug and was about to make a comment about not getting a gift from her daughter when Alex pulled out an apron that announced it was being worn by the greatest chef in the world.

The following morning, Alex was down early for breakfast. Not long after Aurea and Matt came down the stairs into the kitchen.

Rose-Anne was taking breakfast orders and delivering them one at a time.

Aurea said she was looking forward to fishing the next day on the Minnow and asked if Alex was going to fish.

Alex said that she wouldn't miss it. She planned to catch enough fish to make sure there would be plenty for the following day. She smiled and added that all the fish they caught would be cleaned by the new kitchen help that her mother had hired so it would be the right time for each of them to catch their limit.

Matt laughed and said he hoped fishing would be great for all of them.

Rose-Anne said that she too hoped that fishing would be good. She added that she would hate to have to serve pizza.

Russel had been listening to the banter and said that he would prepare all the poles that afternoon and make sure they got on the Minnow. He added that he would put in an order for the bait with Dexter to make sure they had a good variety to choose from.

Matt took Aurea's hand and said that it was time to get to the end of the driveway and catch the bus.

Alex jumped up and said the she was coming too.

Aurea took her hand, and they walked down the lane holding hands. She knew she was one of the luckiest girls in her school. She had parents, grandparents, and close friends all of whom loved her. She thought school was easy and fishing on weekends was grand.

New Direction

As Alex and Matt walked back toward the house, he brought up the fact that the money that Johnnie had mentioned was well beyond anything he had ever dreamt would happen to them. He wondered if she needed to continue her investigative business.

Alex thought for a moment and said that the business certainly would be able to choose only the cases that interested one of the principles, and she could see setting up a charity that they could all get involved in that would fill in the quiet times on the investigation side. She added that she wanted to do more with her charity, "Helping Hands." Part of the settlement was the smuggling operation building and the people that worked there. She planned to turn that into a charity that would seek to help the homeless. She looked at Matt, squeezed his hand and said that she was going to make sure that she focused on him and Aurea more and the business a little less.

Matt gave her a hug and said that it made him feel like he was being listened to.

The next day the fish count on the Minnow hit a record high. The bass seemed to enjoy every type of bait, and everyone caught their limit.

Rose-Anne laughed when Aurea said that they had all celebrated the fact that they did not have to clean their own fish.

Alex added that since her mother would be busy supervising the cleaning of the fish, her father had invited them to the pizza shop for lunch and to his favorite Italian restaurant for dinner.

Rose-Anne said that she would be going to dinner with them and afterwards they should enjoy desert by the pool.

The Sunday fishing trip on the Golden Goose was attended by all the company personnel and their significant others. Nolan had flown in and made the Saturday night desert session and joined in on the Sunday fishing outing. Everyone kept lunch on the light side in anticipation of the evening dinner.

Alex decided that the light lunch had been appropriate because her mother prepared the lake trout and bass in three different fashions. It seemed to her that her mother was becoming a better chef by the day. She listened to everyone say how delicious everything was. By dinner's end the fish had been devoured and everyone was ready for the rhubarb-strawberry pie and the to die for mud pie.

After leaving the new restaurant and going home, she watched Aurea splash around in the pool and felt that she had made the right decision in moving home, buying the marina, and setting up her own investigation agency.

The focus of the evening's pool side discussion was the amazing amount of money the first case for *Evercrest, McGregor, Smith and O'Brien* had pulled in.

She gave Linda and Lorie as the two who were junior partners the credit for getting the case in the door. She added that as soon as the two drew their paintings about the case they were in line for a promotion.

New Direction

The evening by the pool could have lasted for most of the night but they all were still suffering from the pain of being shot and chose to make it a short evening, stand under a hot shower and get a good night's sleep.

On Monday Alex called the team together to review their case and how they were closing it.

She again thanked Linda and Lorie for bringing the Navy smuggling case in the door. She thanked Johnnie for finding out who the king pin of the smuggling operation was and his ability to find the offshore bank accounts and how much money was in each account.

She commented that together they had tracked down Phil and in the end he had tried to kill all of them. She made the point that only one person had not been tracked down and she was not looking to do so. She pointed to Johnnie who had found her and learned she was going to a local college to become a nurse. It appeared that she had decided to seek a more meaningful life. She said that they would keep an eye on her to see that she stuck with her new life.

Cheryl had abandoned being a bodyguard and was currently working in a used bookstore just north of San Francisco. She had enrolled in a local junior college and was working towards a nursing degree and hoped to get accepted at one of the many California state colleges.

She wondered what had happened to Phil. He had given her twenty thousand dollars when she had declined to fly with him to Hawaii. She figured he would be the one that would get chased and she believed he would get caught. She hoped that she was low enough on the totem pole to be ignored. She would have been happy if she could have heard how she was discussed in the meeting that determined her fate. As it was she was happy to be pursuing something that made her life meaningful to her.

Alex pointed out that everyone in the organization would get an equal share.

Marisa asked if everyone included her.

Alex smiled, nodded, and said everyone meant everyone and in this case she was including Darrel who had flown them half way across the world and had helped to capture of Phil. She added that it made all of them very rich and she planned to make sure that the cases that they took on would be of the most challenging kind that were found few and far between. This meant that they would be very bored unless they took on some personal endeavors such as her spending more time focused on her Helping Hands organization and converting Stan's legitimate business into a charity.

Trey spoke up and said that he would love to spend time with the Helping Hands program because he had a lot of history with the property where it was located.

New Direction

Linda smiled and said that she was going to spend a great deal of time living on Maui and getting painting lessons from her mother.

Lorie said that she was going to expand the art gallery in Cincinnati and spend a great deal of time using the companies new yacht trying to make it into a going business like the Golden Goose.

Johnnie added that he planned to take it easy, go out on the Golden Goose as often as possible and eat oatmeal and chocolate chip cookies baked by his most favorite detective.

Marisa said she was amazed and still in shock that she was getting an equal share like everyone else. She said that she had a couple of trips she wanted to take but what she looked forward to the most was working with all of them.

Alex looked around the table and complemented all of them for working so well together and she was sure they would continue to have each other's backs.

The bell from the lobby rang.

Marisa excused herself and went out to see who it might be. She found a rather handsome, young-looking man who introduced himself as Riley Lansberry. He said that he was coming in to be interviewed for the position of pilot of the company plane. Marisa smiled and said that he was just in time and asked him to follow her. She led him back to the main conference room where the interview would take place.

Linda watched as Marisa led a handsome man into the meeting and introduced him as Riley Lansberry who had come to be interviewed for the position of company pilot.

Alex asked if everyone wanted to be part of the interview. Trey, Johnnie, and Lorie all said they were ready for a break and got up and followed Marisa out of the conference room.

Alex welcomed Riley and asked him how long he had been flying. He shared the fact that he had just graduated from flight school. He had flown helicopters in the Navy and had a brief tour in Iraq where he was the pilot for an observation helicopter. He had been lucky not to see any direct fighting. On his return he had immediately entered flight school to be a pilot of commercial jets.

Linda asked him why he should be hired with so little experience.

He shook his head and said that it didn't sound like he was making the right impression. He wanted to make sure that the two of them looked at him as a mature person who would do a great job. His focus was always on safety and making sure that what he was flying was in top condition. He could overhaul most jet engines on the small commercial planes, and he was a pilot not a flight mechanic. His hours flying jet planes was on the low side, but his skill was at the top in his class.

Alex asked him how he knew Darrel Quinly.

New Direction

Riley smiled and said that he was a friend of his older brother. The two of them had attended the University of Illinois. Darrel had been one of the reasons he had enlisted, received a degree, and had become a helicopter pilot and recently had gone on to become qualified to fly commercial jets.

Alex smiled and said that he was indeed making the right impression and that she was hiring him, and his first assignment was to travel to Manila and fly the company's new jet airplane back. He would fly there first class, spend as much time there getting use to the plane as he saw necessary and then flying it back.

Linda smiled and said that she was going to escort him there and then fly back with him. She asked when he was planning to leave for Manila. She had felt an immediate draw to him, and she planned on following through to find out if it was real.

Alex noted the attraction and hoped that Linda had found the person that would make her whole.

The End

New Direction

<u>About the Author</u>

Ronald E. Mueller
remwriter95@gmail.com

Ron grew up in what is now Flint River State Park in Southeast Iowa. The 170-year-old house Ron lived in is built into a hillside. It faces a 125-foot-high cliff towering over the little Flint River. The house and the land talked to him about; the passing of time, the struggle to conquer the land, the struggles people faced and the wonder of nature.

He climbed the cliffs, crawled into the caves, dove from the swimming rock, collected clams from the bottom of the pond, gigged and skinned frogs for their legs. He trapped muskrats for fur, hunted raccoon in the dead of night, and with only a stick hunted rabbits in the dead of winter.

His young life was outdoors, and nature tested him.

He walked to a one room stone schoolhouse uphill both ways. A stern but warm-hearted teacher, Mrs. Henry was instrumental in shaping his character as she shepherded him from the fourth to the eighth grade. A Montessori before its time. It was a great way to grow up.

His experiences inter-twined with snippets of fantasy lend themselves to the adventures he leads the reader through.

Characters in the Story

Alex	Cathy	Evercrest	Cincinnati Police Detective
Matthew	Timothy	Knolton	Alex's suitor
Aurea		Carvalho	Daughter Adopted by Alex
Rose-Anne	Germain	Evercrest	Alex's mother
Russel	Johnson	Evercrest	Alex's father
Trey	Clay	McGregor	Alex's Detective Partner
Lindsey		McGregor	Wife
Nolan		McGregor	Son
Johnnie	Baily	Smith	a major character
Mary		Higgins	Johnnie's mate
Bruce	Lincoln	Johnson	Cincy Chief of Detectives
Mary-Anne	Leslie	Johnson	Chiefs Wife
Bill	Hamilton	Danson	Detective
Travis	Bailey	Carter	Detective
Dr. Rogers			Cincinnati Coroner
Jane	Elousie	Stradford	Lieutenant Governor
Dexter,			Marina owner
Golden Goose			Name of the Yacht
Annie	Lorie	Scots-Obrian	Missing girl
Linda		Scots	Annie's older daughter
Lorie		Scots	Annie's second daughter
Darrel		Quinly	Pilot private jet Brian leased.
Brenda		Langely	Art Dealer
Cais		Leu	Alex's Viet friend
Jane	Elousie	Stradford	Lieutenant Governor
Jason		Shephard	Alex's first boss
Brian	Rory	O'Neill	Main character

New Direction

Kekoa		Ikaika	Hawaiian It
Anela		Kamaka	Kekoa's soul mate
Joe		Brown	RS leader from Cincy
Randolf		Task	IRS agent Texas
Brian		Lexter	Cincy FBI Bureau Chief
Harold		Zimmerman	DEA
Janaina		Carvalho	Mother
Aurea		Carvalho	Daughter
Bento		Carvalho	Father
Fernanda			Grand Mother
Marisa	Kimberly	Eberly	Support in new business
Lydia		Murray	Navy Lieutenant
Lt. Lyle		Halloway	Navy Lieutenant
Darrel		Quinly	Pilot of the private jet.
Capt. Bilan		Kirpatrick	Capt. San Diego Naval Base
Phil		Davidson	Arms Distributor
Ivan		Lubosky	bodyguard # 1
Stan		Newbury	bodyguard # 2
Cheryl		Hinderman	bodyguard # 3
Riley		Lansberry	Alex's new Pilot

Ron Mueller

Published by: Around the World Publishing LLC.

QR Links to
ATWP.US web site

www.ingramcontent.com/pod-product-compliance
Lightning Source LLC
Chambersburg PA
CBHW070550100726
47907CB00004B/1336